DENIM DIARIES: BOOK 2

GROWN IN 60 SECONDS

DENIM DIARIES: BOOK 2

GROWN IN 60 SECONDS

DARRIEN LEE

www.urbanbooks.net

Urban Books
1199 Straight Path
West Babylon, NY 11704

Denim Diaries: Book 2 Grown In 60 Seconds copyright ©
2009 Darrien Lee

ISBN- 13: 978-1-933967-72-1
ISBN- 10: 1-933967-72-2

First Printing April 2009
Printed in the United States of America

10 9 8 7 6 5 4 3 2 1

Distributed by Kensington Publishing Corp.
Submit Wholesale Orders to:
Kensington Publishing Corp.
C/O Penguin Group (USA) Inc.
Attention: Order Processing
405 Murray Hill Parkway
East Rutherford, NJ 07073-2316
Phone: 1-800-526-0275
Fax: 1-800-227-9604

DENIM DIARIES: BOOK 2

GROWN IN 60 SECONDS

Prologue

Denim walked into the funeral parlor and slowly made her way down to the front of the room. She looked around at all the people who had come to pay their last respects to a young man who was obviously loved by many, but who had also caused a lot of sorrow to others. Drugs were something the community was trying to get rid of, so one less thug wouldn't cause city leaders to lose any sleep.

The flowers surrounding the walnut coffin made the whole scene look like something out of a gangster movie. It was the funeral of Carlton Miller, the head of an up and coming gang of thugs. He was murdered days earlier in a seedy section of the city.

Carlton's entourage and close associates sat in

seats behind the family. His mother appeared visibly distraught, along with other members of his family. Could it be that they really loved him, or were the tears because they had lost the major source of their illegal income?

Denim shook her head to clear it. She couldn't believe that the young man lying dead was the same young man who'd been her physical therapy patient. She wasn't one to judge, but it did hurt her to find out that Carlton could've put her life in danger by being in close proximity to her at least three days a week. She'd become quite close to him, and was actually starting to become attracted to him—until the unthinkable happened.

The crowd of people in front of her slowly moved forward as soft gospel music played throughout the room. Denim's heart was starting to accelerate as she waited in the long line to view Carlton's body. It all felt like a bad dream, and she wanted to get out of there as soon as possible.

The air felt as if it had become thinner by the time she made her way to the front of the line and slowly leaned forward to gaze inside the casket. The sight of Carlton lying dead in front of her made her sick to her stomach and a little lightheaded. As she stared at his face, she thought that the mortician had done an excellent job making him presentable for the viewing. Before walking away, Denim reached over and gently touched Carlton's hand and whispered, "Rest in peace, Carlton."

Just as she was about to turn around and leave, a young male who was standing next to her pulled out a large caliber weapon and, in slow motion, pumped three bullets into Carlton's already lifeless body. The sound was deafening, and the room erupted in total chaos as mourners screamed and stampeded toward the exits.

Chairs were flying every which way, and Denim realized she was caught up in a déjà vu moment. Unable to move, she stood frozen in her spot, until a strong hand yanked her body out of harm's way.

Denim screamed as she woke up out of her dream. Her parents came running into her bedroom and turned on the light just as Denim sat up in bed.

"Denim, are you okay?" her mother asked as she sat on the side of her daughter's bed.

With tears in her eyes, she answered, "I'm fine, Momma. I just had a bad dream."

Her father walked around the room and checked the windows to make sure they were secure. This was something he did often before going to bed, but it didn't hurt to check them again.

"Honey, you're safe. What were you dreaming about?"

Denim wiped the tears from her eyes and lied. "I can't remember, Daddy, but whatever it was, it was horrible."

Valessa caressed her daughter's arm to comfort her. "It must have been a horrible dream for you to scream like that. You almost gave me a heart attack."

"I'm sorry, Momma. I didn't mean to scare you guys."

Samuel kissed her forehead and said, "Don't worry about it. We've all had our share of bad dreams. Just know that you're safe and you have nothing to worry about."

Denim placed her hand over her racing heart and said, "Thank you, Daddy."

"Can I get you anything before you go back to sleep?" he asked.

Denim shook her head and tried her best to smile. "No, I'm fine. Thank you."

Valessa caressed her daughter's face before she stood and tightened the belt on her robe. Denim could see the worried look on her mother's face as she pulled the comforter over her body.

"You guys don't have to worry. I'll be okay. I'm

going to try to go back to sleep now, so you can go back to your bedroom."

Feeling somewhat hesitant to leave her, Valessa asked, "Are you sure you don't want me to hang around until you fall asleep?"

"No, I'm good. Honest," she answered to reassure her parents.

"Okay, sweetie. Good night."

Denim nodded to her parents with a smile on her face.

"Good night."

After her parents left the bedroom, Denim turned off the light and hugged her pillows. Her dream was so vivid, but she didn't want to tell her parents about it because if they knew, they wouldn't let her attend Carlton's funeral for sure. They were already reluctant because of his shady background. It was going to be a long night, and Denim knew sleep wouldn't come easy.

Chapter One

Denim woke up the next morning and got dressed for a job interview. She was interviewing for an intern position at a new physical therapy clinic located across from the hospital where she used to work. Her plan was to attend Carlton's funeral once she finished her interview, so she could pay her last respects. She had to admit to herself that after her bizarre dream, she was a little nervous about going, but she wouldn't feel right if she didn't go.

Carlton was known on the streets as Li'l Carl. He had been shot months earlier at a birthday party hosted by Denim's boyfriend, André Patterson. At the time of the shooting, he was the leader of a dangerous teenage gang; however, Denim had no knowledge of his ruthless activities. To her, he was just another teen, and when he became her patient after the shooting, she still had no clue that he was the infamous Li'l Carl she'd heard about. All she knew was that he'd been shot and needed her help. While working together in physical therapy, they'd become quite close, and they were beginning to become even closer until he was gunned down. Today was going to be bittersweet, and she had a little anxiety about attending the services, but she knew she had to go.

Denim completed her job interview and made it to the chapel just in time. As she sat there, she noticed a crowd of young men seated behind the family. She suspected they were part of Carlton's crew.

The funeral services were short and sweet. When she viewed Carlton's body, he looked like he was sleeping. Another young life wasted senselessly. As Denim turned and made her way toward the exit, she noticed a familiar face. As she filed out of the chapel with the rest of the crowd, she came face to face with her dear friend, DeMario González. DeMario was born in the United States one year after his family migrated from Venezuela. He was an extremely handsome seventeen-year-old with a tan skin tone and exotic features.

She hugged him lovingly and said, "Hey, De-Mario."

"Hey, Denim, what's been up?" he asked as he released her.

"Nothing much. School, working, playing football . . . you know, the usual. You have no idea how glad I am to see you, though."

DeMario bumped his shoulders against hers playfully and said, "Is that right? You look good."

She reached down and held his hand and said, "Thank you. You look good yourself."

Denim was dressed in a black, two-piece linen suit with a short skirt, which revealed her shapely legs. DeMario had on a pair of baggy jeans and a blue-and-white button-down dress shirt. His white Nike athletic shoes finished off his ensemble.

"I hate funerals. What brought you down here today?" she asked.

"I knew there would be a lot of people hanging out, so I thought I would check it out. What about you? This is not particularly your crowd of people or neighborhood."

Denim started to get emotional as tears welled up in her eyes.

"Carlton was one of my patients. I worked with him in the physical therapy clinic after he got shot.

I didn't know he was the notorious Li'l Carl until after he died. He was so nice. He didn't seem like the kind of guy who would be involved in gangs. I actually liked him. He made me laugh."

DeMario nodded as he listened to Denim speak highly of the young, deceased brother. She'd never associated herself with people like Li'l Carl, but she never was one to judge people or think she was better than anyone. Her parents had taught her that much.

"Whatever you say, but girls like you can get caught up with these so-called 'nice' guys. Believe me; Li'l Carl had a dark side."

She looked away from him in silence as his words sunk in. She understood that DeMario knew what he was talking about. He'd grown up in a rough part of the city and knew the personalities of gangbangers and drug dealers.

"Listen, I'm sorry dude is dead, but I'm glad you didn't get mixed up with him. Li'l Carl was a major player, and it's only a matter of time before his crew gets revenge. It's going to be like Dodge City around here, so make sure you watch your back."

"I hear you, but it sounds like we're talking about two different people."

"That's what I'm talking about. Guys like Li'l

Carl can be deceiving. That's how they suck you into their world, and that's how they make their money."

"All of this is so hard to believe. I never would've dreamed that he could be the head of some gang."

At that moment, a cold sweat broke out on her brow and her breathing became erratic. She put her hand over her chest and leaned against De-Mario's shoulder. "I can't breathe, DeMario. I need to get out of here."

DeMario took Denim by the hand and led her away from the crowd of people who continued to mingle around the chapel, even though the funeral procession had already pulled away from the curb. The atmosphere was taking on a block party appeal as they made their way through the crowd. Once they cleared the cluster of onlookers, the pair found a bench in front of a convenience store half a block down the street from the chapel.

After sitting down, he asked, "Is this better?"

"Yes, this is much better. You've always been a good friend to me, DeMario. I miss hanging out with you."

DeMario grinned as he pulled a pack of gum out of his pocket. He offered her a piece, but she waved him off. He popped a piece of gum into his mouth and said, "You've been my friend too. I know it's been hard since I changed schools. It also don't help that you and Patrice are still not speaking."

"Well, I can't help that," she answered as she pulled a flyer off the window and read it. It was obvious that the mention of Patrice's name made her uncomfortable. Silence fell over the pair for a few seconds as they watched patrons go in and out of the store. The smell of barbeque was in the air as smoke billowed from a large barrel-style barbeque grill in front of the store.

"I bet Patrice would have a fit if she knew you were sitting here talking to me."

"Patrice don't run me or pick my friends."

"Yeah, right," she teased as she stuck the flyer back on the window.

"I'm serious, sis," DeMario replied. "She knows I don't play."

"You're fooling yourself. If Patrice said jump, you'd probably ask her how high."

"Bull!" DeMario yelled. "You've lost your damn mind."

Denim giggled and playfully punched him in the arm. "Stop cursing. You just got out of church."

"No, you just got out of church. I was on the outside looking in. I can't believe you even said that bullshit."

Denim giggled again. "You just can't stop cursing, can you?"

The pair burst out laughing.

DeMario had been one part of their foursome of friends. The others were her boyfriend, Dré, who mysteriously disappeared, and DeMario's girlfriend, Patrice, who got pregnant, causing Denim to become distant, hurt, and angry. She felt that Patrice had ruined the plans they'd had for years to go off to college together. Her relationship with Patrice had ended abruptly after being close friends practically all their lives. It had been months since they had seen or spoken to each other.

Dré and his family had left town without so much as a good-bye, and no one knew where they were or why they disappeared so suddenly. Denim hoped that DeMario would be able to tell her where Dré was and why he had to leave.

Both situations left her feeling very alone, but seeing DeMario again had lifted her spirits and warmed her heart. It felt like old times.

"DeMario, did you ever find out why Dré left town or where he's living?"

DeMario looked over at her and hesitated before

answering. "I'd rather not say." What DeMario was trying not to do was break a promise to his friend.

"You'd rather not say?" she asked as she turned toward him. "So you do know something?"

"I can't say," he answered as he spit his gum out into a nearby trash bin.

Denim angrily grabbed his arm. "Do you even care what I've been through since he left?"

"I can imagine."

"Can you?"

Denim had been an emotional wreck since Dré and his family disappeared. She thought she would never get through the pain of losing her first and only love. The pain had eased up slightly in his absence, but it had left a huge void and sense of emptiness in her heart.

"I'm not stupid. I know how much you love Dré. He's my best friend, remember?"

She let out a breath and said, "Yes, I remember. So do you know where he is or not?"

He put his arm around her shoulders and pulled her close. "Denim, I love you, but Dré is like a brother to me, and one thing I can't do is put his business on blast without his permission."

Denim pushed away from him and stood. DeMario could see the steam of anger rising from her jacket, and her complexion had darkened from the anger. He knew he had hit a nerve with her, but a promise was a promise.

"Don't be pissed off with me. If you were in my shoes, you'd do the same thing. I just wish you would trust me."

"Why should I trust you? You don't trust me enough to tell me about Dré."

DeMario lowered his head. He found himself wedged between his two best friends, and he didn't know what to do.

"I have to go, DeMario. It was great seeing you again."

As she turned to walk away, DeMario grabbed her arm. "Wait! Just wait a minute!"

She looked into his weary eyes and saw his frustration. "Why?"

"Okay, if I tell you something, you have to promise—and I mean promise—to keep it to yourself. This is nothing to play with, Denim. I mean it."

She touched his face and said, "You know anything you tell me is safe."

"It better be, because if you let me down, don't ever expect me to trust you again. Do you feel me?"

Happy, she said, "I feel you."

DeMario took Denim by the hand once again and said, "Cool. Now, follow me."

"Follow you? I thought you said you was going to tell me about Dré. Where are we going?"

He gave her hand a squeeze and said, "You'll see."

"Is that the best answer you can give me?"

"You said you wanted to know about Dré. Now's your chance."

She pointed across the street and the chapel parking lot and asked, "But what about my car?"

"Come on. You can drive. You can bring me back to my truck later."

They crossed the street together and walked over to her car. She unlocked the doors and put her hands on her hips. "How long will this take? I told my parents I would be home right after the funeral."

DeMario climbed into the passenger's seat and put on his seatbelt. "You said you wanted to know what's up, so call your parents and tell them you'll be a little later than expected."

"What should I tell them? You know my dad can smell a lie a mile away."

"Is your old man still clocking you like five-O?"

Denim giggled as she buckled her seatbelt. "He's not so bad."

"Please! Yes he is. I don't know how you and Dré ever got a chance to—"

Denim held up her hand. "Don't say it, DeMario. I don't want to think about that right now."

"You still love him, don't you?"

She nodded before starting up her car. "Of course I still love him. I'll always love Dré, but I'm here and he's God knows where. End of story."

DeMario smiled and said, "He still loves you too."

"You think?"

"No, I don't think, I know," he announced. "He tells me all the time."

Hearing DeMario say those words sent a warm sensation through her body. She wanted to believe that Dré still loved her, but after not hearing from him for so long, she wondered if he really did; yet she was still hopeful that he would come back so they could be a couple again.

"You wouldn't lie to me, would you?"

"No, I wouldn't lie to you," he answered. "Dré misses you, and I can't believe you think I would lie about that."

"I'm sorry. It's just that it hurts too much to talk about him."

"He's hurting too."

You've seen him?" she asked as she drove through town. "Where is he?"

DeMario looked through Denim's CDs, slid one into CD player and turned up the volume without answering.

She turned the music down and glanced over at him. "You're avoiding my question."

"I can't answer you right now," he replied just as a car full of a group of about five teenage boys pulled up beside them at the next traffic light. The driver made eye contact with DeMario and nodded his head at him. DeMario nodded back and watched them as they continued down the street ahead of them.

Denim noticed the vehicle because the driver raised and lowered it on hydraulics as he drove away. "They look rough."

DeMario laughed and said, "You're with me, girl. Ain't nobody gonna mess with you. They know me around here."

"Who are they? I've never seen them at my school. Do they go to school with you?"

DeMario laughed again. "They don't go to school, girl. They're gangbangers.

"I guess you would know," she joked.

DeMario laughed. He knew she was joking because he was nowhere close to being a gangbanger. He wore the baggy jeans like all the boys did at their age, but he carried himself like a respectable young man.

Seconds later, his cell phone rang. He looked down at it but didn't answer it. Instead, he tucked it inside his pocket.

"Was that Patrice?"

"Yes, that was your best friend," he teased.

"Best friend? You and I both know that Patrice and I haven't been best friends in a long time now."

"Don't be like that, Denim." He shook his head. "You two need to squash the drama and let it go. Both of you are so damn stubborn."

"It's her fault! . . . But forget about that right now. I want to know where we're going."

"Go out to the lake. I'm supposed to meet Dré."

Denim's head snapped around, causing the car to swerve slightly.

DeMario sat up abruptly and yelled, "Keep your eyes on the road!"

"Are you serious? You're taking me to see Dré? So you do know where he is?"

"Okay! Yeah, we keep in touch from time to time, but only when it's safe."

She gripped the steering wheel in anger. "He can keep in touch with you but not me? You call that love?" she asked sarcastically as she turned off the main road into the park leading to the lake.

"Ease up on the gas pedal! You took that turn on two wheels!"

She shook her head in disbelief. "I can't believe it. Dré can keep in touch with you but not me."

DeMario leaned back in his seat and briefly closed his eyes. "Listen, Denim. I knew that Li'l Carl was one of your patients and so did Dré. He asked me look after you. He said he saw you kiss the dude one day and thought something crazy might happen at the funeral, so he asked me to shadow you if you showed up."

"That kiss was nothing and I told him so. If he was so concerned about me, why couldn't he come himself?"

"He wanted to, but the risk was too high."

Frustrated, Denim asked, "What's really going on? Why did they have to leave town?"

DeMario looked Denim in the eyes without responding.

"Cool," she said. "If that's the way you want to be, fine. I'll ask him myself. Where are you supposed to meet him?"

"We're meeting at the usual spot," he answered.

Denim remembered exactly where the usual spot was as she drove through the park. She'd spent many nights there as a couple with Dré and as a group with Patrice and DeMario.

"If Dré had any control over what was going on with him and his family, he would be with you."

She turned down a narrow road and said, "You always defend him."

"I'm not going to argue with you. Just chill and question Dré when you see him. I'm out of it."

DeMario received a text message on his cell phone. He read it and then quickly typed in a response just as Denim brought her car to halt. She put the car in park and looked out toward the lake.

"Now what?"

"We wait," he replied.

"How long?"

DeMario smiled. "Not long. We're a little early."

Denim shifted in her seat and pulled her cell phone out of her purse. "I need to call my parents."

DeMario laughed. "Damn, your parents are strict. Dré's a good one, because most guys couldn't handle dealing with your ol' man."

"They've loosened up a little bit since Dré left. All I have time for now is school, cheerleading, and work."

He shook his head in disbelief and changed the subject. "I really wish you and Patrice would stop being so damn stubborn and set aside your differences."

"Stop calling me stubborn!" she yelled. "I'm no more stubborn than Patrice."

"You're right. You and Patrice need to get over yourselves."

She looked over at DeMario and then pinched his upper arm.

"Ouch! That hurt!"

"That's what you get for calling me stubborn."

"Damn, Denim!" he yelled as he rubbed his arm.

"Where's Dré ? Because I have to go."

DeMario started bouncing his head to the music booming from the CD player. "He'll be here."

Denim's heart was starting to beat harder in her chest. Her palms were sweaty, and it was getting harder for her to swallow. The anxiety of seeing Dré was getting the best of her, but she had no choice but to wait.

Chapter Two

Fifteen minutes later, DeMario looked at his watch and then opened the car door.

"It's time. Come on, let's walk."

He walked around to open Denim's door. The fresh scent of the lake and the wildflowers surrounding it quickly brought back memories of the times she'd spent there. Nothing had changed. If anything, the scenery had gotten even more beautiful.

She took his hand, but before stepping out of the car, she stopped and looked down at her feet. "I can't walk around out here in these heels."

DeMario looked down and joked, "I know you don't expect me to carry you."

At that moment, Dré stepped out from behind a tree and said, "Nah, bro, that's my job. Besides, I would hate for Denim to mess up those beautiful shoes."

"Dré?" she whispered as her eyes widened at the sight of him. Dré was even finer than the last time she'd seen him, but today, he made her heart thump in her chest and fireworks go off in her head. When he smiled at her, it seemed to light up the sky, making tears well up in her eyes.

"What a nice surprise, Cocoa Princess. You are a sight for sore eyes."

He'd called her by the pet name he'd given her, and she was left speechless. Her heart was telling her to jump into his arms and kiss him senseless, but her legs and arms remained frozen.

As he walked closer to her, the nearness of his tall, muscular frame made it harder for her to breathe. Just as he leaned over to kiss her, she turned away from him, denying him the opportunity.

Surprised by her response, he took a step back and studied her. "Oh, it's like that? I thought you would be happy to see me."

Denim cleared the dryness out of her throat and said, "I am glad to see you, but how can you step to me like this without so much as a letter or a telephone call?"

He slid his hands inside his pockets and said, "I have my reasons."

Excuses, excuses. His response seemed typical of a lot of guys, and it angered her.

Dré could see that Denim wasn't going for a lame excuse, so he did his best to explain. "Sweetheart, you know I must be jammed up in bad situation if I haven't contacted you."

"Do I? You haven't told me anything, so how would I know about your situation?"

He reached down and gently rubbed the back of her hand. "I was hoping that you would be a little more understanding."

"I can't do this," she said as she pulled her hand away and backed away from him. "You're playing with my heart and it's not fair. What do you expect me to do, wait on you? Hell to the no!"

Dré frowned. He expected her to be upset, but he didn't want to lose her, and he'd do whatever he could to keep that from happening. He didn't have much time, but he needed privacy to talk to her.

"DeMario, could you give us a minute?" he asked.

DeMario tugged on his baggy jeans and slid off the trunk of the car.

"No problem, bro. I'll be down at the lake if you need some backup."

Denim and Dré watched as DeMario walked down the narrow dirt trail toward the lake. Once he was out of sight, Dré pointed to a nearby picnic bench.

"We need to talk."

Denim walked over to the bench in silence and took a seat. As Dré watched her movements, he couldn't help but stare at her heavenly body. Her suit wasn't revealing, but it still showed the shapely curves of her hips and thighs. Her smooth brown skin and soft hair made his heart ache. He missed her so much.

Once she was seated, she lit into him before he had a chance to say anything. She pointed her finger in his face and fired off on him. "Listen, Dré, the only thing we need to talk about is what's really going on with you. Otherwise, we have nothing to talk about. I'm getting sick and tired of you popping in and out of my life. You're playing with my heart like you don't love me at all. I gave myself to you and only you. That used to mean something to you."

Her words hit hard. She had given him her most

precious gift, and he could see why she would feel like he was stringing her along. He lowered his head and softly pleaded for mercy. "Denim, you have no idea what I've risked to come here today. If my dad ever finds out, he's gonna go ballistic."

"So is this about your dad or you?"

"I can't say."

"You don't seem to have a problem putting De-Mario and his family in danger by contacting him. What's the difference?"

"It's not that simple. DeMario can take care of things if something jumps off."

"Oh, and I can't?" she yelled back at him.

Frustrated, he grabbed her chin and made her look into his eyes. "This is not a game! People could get killed. Can't you understand that I don't want anything to happen to you?"

Stunned by his sudden reaction, she couldn't hold back her emotions any longer. Dré's eyes were full of the fire and passion she was accustomed to, and it made her weak.

Denim's voice cracked as she leaned against his strong body. "I don't want anything to happen to you either, but I think after all we've been to each other, I deserve to know the truth."

He hugged her lovingly and said, "Too many people are already at risk, so if you have to hate me for not telling you, go right ahead."

She kissed his chin and said, "I could never hate you, but I do hate this situation."

He pulled Denim into his lap and wrapped his arms around her waist. "Believe me, I do."

The young couple held each other for what seemed like an eternity. As they sat there, the chirping birds sang a sweet, harmonious song just for them.

Dré slid his hand up her thigh and said, "Having you in my arms right now is driving me crazy. You have no idea how bad I want to be with you."

She nuzzled his warm neck and said, "I think you'd better stop before you get something started."

He stopped caressing her body and slowly lowered his lips to hers. His mouth toyed with hers before he deepened their kiss.

When Denim opened her eyes, she saw everlasting love in Dré's eyes. They stared at each other for several seconds as they both reminisced about their forbidden, yet fiery rendezvous. The memories caused her lower body to melt and cloud her head.

"What now?" he asked.

"You tell me."

"You're my girl and you're going to always be my girl, so no more talk about moving on. Cool?"

"Cool," she happily repeated.

"I do love you, Denim."

"I love you too."

Tears spilled out of Denim's eyes as they stood. He wiped the tears off her cheeks and caressed her shoulders. His hands slowly made their way down to her curvy backside, where he caressed and massaged her hips.

"It's hard not being able to touch you like this."

"Dré you're torturing me," she said breathlessly.

"I'll work something out," he answered before lowering his lips to hers once again. His kiss was firm and sweet, and Denim never wanted it to end. But unfortunately, it had to. He yelled for DeMario, and they watched him as he sent a text on his cell phone.

"Are y'all cool?" he asked.

Denim blushed and hugged Dré's waist. "Yeah, we're cool."

"Good. You guys need to hurry up and say your good-byes because I have to roll out."

Denim put her hands on her hips and said, "We're hurrying, DeMario! Okay?"

DeMario laughed as he opened the car door and turned up the music.

Dré walked Denim over to her car and opened the door for her. "DeMario's right. He needs to get home, and so do you."

Holding onto him tighter, she whispered, "I don't want to let you go."

Dré smiled and said, "I don't want to let you go either. I'll see you soon. Now, give me a kiss."

She happily tiptoed and wrapped her arms around his neck, giving him one last long, sultry kiss. DeMario pushed the car horn, startling the couple apart.

Chapter Three

As soon as DeMario stepped inside the door, a small object flew past his head. He immediately ducked, not knowing exactly what it was.

"What the hell? Damn, Patrice! What's wrong with you?" he asked as he picked up a small teddy bear off the floor.

Patrice's mother, Felicia Fontenot, said, "Don't curse in my house, DeMario."

"I'm sorry, Mrs. Felicia."

"Apology accepted."

"You need to be apologizing to me instead of Momma!" Patrice yelled as she stood in the middle of the floor in a short red maternity jumpsuit. Patrice had a huge stomach, but everything else on her stayed the same size, including her legs.

"Where have you been?" she asked angrily.

Felicia looked up from her *Ebony* magazine and with a stern voice, she yelled, "Sit down, Patrice, before you make yourself go into early labor. Now, apologize to DeMario!"

She looked over at her mother and pointed at DeMario. "Momma, he's the one who owes me an apology!"

Felicia closed the magazine, swung her honey-blond, wavy micro braids over her shoulders, and asked, "For what, child?"

Patrice walked over to her mother and said, "While I'm sitting here about to explode, he's out having fun with God knows who!"

DeMario shook his head in disbelief. "Come on, Patrice. You're starting to get crazy." He obviously wasn't used to being around pregnant women. One minute Patrice was fine, and the next minute she'd be crying. Little did he know that this emotional rollercoaster would last even months after the baby was born.

Mrs. Fontenot looked over at DeMario with a suspicious eye as she slowly approached him. "DeMario, are you cheating on my daughter?"

He slid his hands in his pockets and said, "No, ma'am. I would never disrespect Patrice like that."

She turned to her pouting daughter. "Patrice, do

you honestly believe that DeMario would do that to you, especially now?"

Her eyes met DeMario's briefly before she looked over at her mother. "I guess not."

"Then stop creating unnecessary drama. You need to stay calm for the baby's sake and for mine," she announced as she walked back over to her chair and picked up her magazine.

Patrice had a reputation for being short-tempered. Since becoming pregnant with DeMario's child, her temper had become even shorter.

DeMario looked at his cell phone and said, "It's my mom. I'll be back in a second."

Felicia and Patrice watched as DeMario walked out of the room and into the kitchen so he could talk in private.

"Little girl, you'd better stop nagging that boy. You can't expect him to be right under you twenty-four-seven. He's going to school and holding down a job, so you need to give him a break. If you keep it up, you're going to run him away."

Patrice plopped down on the sofa and rubbed her stomach. "I'm sorry, Momma."

"I'm not the one you need to apologize to," she commented as she continued to thumb through the magazine without looking up.

DeMario walked back into the room and said, "Excuse me, Mrs. Fontenot. Is it okay if I talk to Patrice in the kitchen?"

"Go right ahead. I'm finished with her," she replied.

Patrice looked over at her mother before allowing DeMario to help her off the sofa.

Once inside the kitchen, he asked, "Why are you trying to hurt me, Patrice, and why would you think I would cheat on you?"

She pointed at him and said, "First of all, if I was trying to hurt your Latino ass, you would be dead. But I love you, so I guess I have to let you live."

DeMario pulled a chair out for her to sit down. He sat down next to her. "Stop cursing, Patrice. I don't want my baby coming out acting ghetto."

She giggled. "Are you calling me ghetto?"

He held her hand and said, "You said it, not me."

They laughed together.

"Seriously, Patrice, do you honestly think I would mess around on you?"

"I don't think you would, but I see how those hoochies look at you, and here I am fat and pregnant. I wouldn't blame you if you did step out on me. I feel so ugly."

DeMario held his hand up to stop her. "You're not ugly. Listen, Patrice, I can't stop girls from checking me out. You're the only one I want; you're the one I love, and you're the one who's having *my baby*. If I didn't love you, I wouldn't be here, period. Understand?"

She nodded and smiled. "Yes, I understand."

"Good," he replied as he leaned forward and caressed her stomach.

"So, where have you been?" she asked. "You've been gone for a long time."

DeMario continued to caress and kiss her stomach. "I was with Denim and Dré," he replied casually.

She pushed away from him. "Excuse me? I can understand Dré, but why Denim?"

DeMario stood and pulled two bottles of water out of the refrigerator. "Chill, baby."

"Why do I have to chill? You're the one who spent the day with my nemesis."

DeMario burst out laughing and nearly spit out his water. "Do you hear yourself? We just straightened out one thing, and now you jumped right into something else. Denim is not your enemy. Besides, you know we're still friends, and she used to be your best friend." Patrice was DeMario's heart, but he would never let her dictate who he could be friends with.

She opened the bottled water and took a sip. "You're right about one thing, she *used to be* my best friend."

"Denim's my friend, and there's nothing you can do about it, so get over it. And you know Dré's my boy, so I'll help him no matter what. It would help the situation and me if you and Denim could find a way to let go of this stupid feud between you two and try to get along."

"Not happening," she quickly replied. "And you tell Dré that I said to leave you out of his little meet-and-greet sessions with Denim."

"You're mean, Patrice. That baby's going to come out with a lot of attitude."

"I'm not mean; I'm real and I tell it like it is," she replied while snapping her finger. "Denim cut me out of her life, and she hasn't had the decency to apologize to me. She's no friend of mine."

"You're loco, Patrice," he said as he reached into his pocket and pulled out a wad of cash.

Patrice's eyes widened at the sight of the money. "I assume you got paid today."

He counted the money without looking at her. "Are you up for shopping for a baby bed?"

She puckered her lips and said, "I would love to."

He tucked the money into his pocket and asked, "Can you believe we're going to have a Venezuelan, Creole, African American baby?"

"That is pretty cool. I wonder who *she's* going to look like."

"Don't you mean *he*?"

"Whatever! I don't care either way, as long as the baby is healthy."

Patrice and DeMario had picked out both boy and girl names for their baby. Unlike many teen parents, they decided not to find out the sex of the baby so they could be surprised.

He reached over and momentarily played with the emerald birthstone ring he'd placed on her finger for Christmas. It would be the birthstone of their child.

"I love you, Patrice."

"I love you too, DeMario."

Their eyes briefly met. He kissed her lips and then her stomach one more time before making their way out to the car and to the shopping center.

Denim pulled into her driveway and found her father standing on the front porch. His expression revealed a look she'd seen before. It was a look of parental relief. Denim exited the vehicle and walked up to the porch.

"Hi, Daddy. Are you out here waiting for me?"

He embraced her and said, "Not really. I was checking the mailbox. How was the job interview?"

"It was great. I'm sure I'll get it."

He released her and sat down in the chair. As he scanned through the mail, he asked, "Did you go to the funeral?"

She looked at her father and sighed. "Yes, I went. It was so sad."

Samuel Mitchell looked over at his daughter, who was now sitting next to him. As she scanned through department store ads, he asked, "Are you okay?"

Denim closed the advertisement. "I think so."

"I can tell something's bothering you, sweetheart. You do know you can talk to me about anything, don't you?"

Denim smiled and rolled her eyes. "Are you sure, Daddy? Even sex?"

He lowered his head and softly answered, "Yes, as painful as it can be for me, even sex."

"I'm just teasing you. But seriously, there is something that I need to tell you."

He braced himself for whatever she could possibly reveal to him.

"Carlton was also known by the name Li'l Carl."

"I know that name. Where have I heard that name before?" he asked.

"He was the teenager who got shot at Dré's birthday party."

Samuel sat up and asked, "That was your patient? Why didn't you tell me?"

Denim lowered her head.

"I read in the newspaper that he was the leader of a teenage gang. Why wouldn't you tell us something like that?"

"At the time I didn't know he was the same person, Daddy. Besides, I didn't find out until after he was killed."

Samuel couldn't do anything but sit and absorb the frightening information that his daughter had just revealed to him. He understood that people who worked in the medical field didn't get to choose who they treated, but this was his daughter, the love of his life. She could've been hurt or killed if a rival gang member showed up at the clinic to take revenge on Carlton and Denim got caught in the crossfire.

"Daddy, why do you have that look on your face?" His eyes had slightly teared up.

"I'm sorry, darling. I was just thinking about what could've happened to you if something had gone bad."

She hugged his neck and pressed her face against his warm neck. "I know I should've told you and Momma, but I had to go to his funeral because from what I saw, he really was a nice guy."

"Denim, when people live those types of lives, they have to take on more than one personality so they can blend into society to do their dirty work. You can't let yourself be fooled for a second because as soon as you let your guard down, that's when you get hurt or killed. Do you understand me?"

"Yes, sir."

Samuel had grown up around gangs, and by the grace of God and strong family support, he was able to steer clear of them. Of course, there were moments he was tempted to join them, but he knew there was no way his parents would let him get away with it. They had plans for him to stay alive, finish high school and college, so he would have chance for a successful and financially secure life in order to start his own family.

"You really should've told us about him when you first found out." Samuel shook his head and stacked up the mail.

She hugged her father's neck."I know. Do you forgive me?"

Samuel put his arm around his daughter's shoulder and kissed her forehead. "I forgive you, baby girl, but next time, tell me. Okay?"

"I will, Daddy."

The father-daughter bond had been mended, and it always felt good to both of them. As expected, there would always be ups and downs in their relationship because of the trials and tribulations of being a teenager and raising one. Denim and her parents had experienced their share of bumps in the road, but they always seemed to smooth things out with love and understanding.

"I'm glad we have an understanding, because there was a time when you made it hard for me and your mother to trust you, especially when Dré was around. He had a big influence on you."

Denim softly whispered, "I know, but Dré's not around anymore."

Denim's father was correct with his observation. Denim loved Dré so much that when he said jump, she asked how high. She was that much in love with him.

"I'm not saying that Dré's not a good kid," Samuel said. "What I'm saying is that you didn't always make the right decisions when it came to him. You two were moving too fast way too soon."

Samuel's heart thumped hard in his chest when he spoke of Dré. The path the young couple was on wasn't one he wanted to think too much about. Dré was actually a little older than Samuel had been when he started exploring his own sexuality, and he knew exactly how the mind of a teenage boy worked. He saw how Dré looked at Denim, his eyes full of hot-blooded passion, all directed at his baby girl.

"Daddy, I can't help it that I fell in love with Dré."

He kissed her forehead again and said, "There will be other boys."

"There's nobody like Dré. I can't see myself with anybody else."

Samuel didn't want to push the issue with her. He knew what he was talking about, and it was clear that his daughter would have to find out the hard way.

"If you say so, sweetheart. Now, come on inside so you can eat dinner."

Denim linked her arm with his and said, "I'm glad, because I'm starving."

He let her enter the house ahead of him."Your mother will be happy to hear that. You haven't had much of an appetite over the past few months. We were worried about you."

Denim stepped into the foyer and turned to her father. She didn't want to tell him that her appetite was back only because she'd seen, touched, and most of all tasted Dré.

Instead, she lied. "I'm okay, Daddy," she assured him. "I know I'm going to get the job at the clinic, so I know I have to keep my body, mind, and spirit sharp."

He laughed at her newfound enthusiasm.

"I can't wait to tell Momma about my interview. It's more money than what I was making at the hospital, and it's closer to school."

"We're all for you working, as long as it doesn't interfere with your grades."

"Thank you, Daddy," she replied. "I'm going upstairs to change my clothes before dinner. Tell Momma I'll be down in a second."

He patted his stomach and said, "Don't be long. I'm kind of hungry myself."

Once in her room, Denim did something she hadn't done in a while: She opened her nightstand and pulled out her denim diary. She turned to a blank page and began to write.

Dear Diary,

I know it's been a long time since I wrote anything, but I haven't had a reason to until today. First of all, I went to a job interview. I must say that I did great. I think the doctors were impressed with me, so hopefully I'll get the job. I'll be making more money—cha-ching!—and the hours are just right.

After the interview, I went to Carlton's funeral. It was sad. No matter what people say about him, he was cool.

The best news I have to report is that I ran into my dear friend, DeMario. It was great seeing him, and it made me realize just how much I miss hanging out with him. The big surprise came when he took me to see Dré! I had no idea when or if I'd ever see him again,

*and he was a beautiful sight for my sore
eyes. He's still super fine, and I nearly passed
out when he put his hands on me. When he
kissed me, I thought I was going to die. It felt
soooo good. God knows I love that man!*

Later!
D

She closed her diary and put it back into her
nightstand. Minutes later, she received a strange
text on her cell phone. When she looked at it, she
didn't recognize the sender or understand the message:

KNOWING THE TRUTH MEANS ACCEPTING THE LIES
FROM THE ONE YOU LOVE.

Denim stared at the message. As her heart immediately started beating wildly in her chest, she
realized it must be from Dré. With her fingers trembling, she typed a response. It was one of her favorite scriptures:

LET HIM HAVE ALL YOUR WORRIES AND CARES,
FOR HE IS ALWAYS THINKING ABOUT YOU AND WATCH-

ING EVERYTHING THAT CONCERNS YOU. 1 PETER 5:7. MY LOVE WILL ALWAYS BE UNCONDITIONAL, BUT I NEED YOU TO TRUST ME AND HELP ME UNDERSTAND THE LIES.

She stared at the LCD screen on her cell phone and anxiously waited for a reply. From downstairs, her parents called her for dinner.

"I'll be there in a second," she yelled.

Her face was hot. She wanted to receive a reply so badly, but still nothing. Moments later, she heard her mother's footsteps come up the stairs and toward her room.

"Come on, Dré, text me back," she whispered as she tried to will her cell phone to respond.

Her mother pushed open the door and asked, "What's taking you so long? I have dinner on the table. Everything's getting cold."

She set her cell phone on the bed and started unbuttoning her blouse. "I'm sorry, Momma. I promise I'll be right down."

Valessa looked at her daughter curiously. "Is something wrong?"

"No, everything's fine. I just got caught up with texting."

"Okay, you have two minutes or we're starting without you," she replied as she backed out of the room.

As soon as her mother closed the door, Denim picked up her cell phone and looked down at the screen. It was blank; still no response. She let out a breath and finished changing her clothes before joining her parents at the dinner table. Unbeknownst to Denim, her cell phone quietly vibrated minutes later with a very special text message response.

Chapter Four

Dré sat on the stone wall in his backyard and threw the basketball as hard as he could against the backside of their brick house. It was a modest home on a tree-lined street in a family-oriented suburb. The houses were filled with upper middle classes families, and the home was much larger than the one they used to have.

Dana Patterson exited the back door and gave Dré a look of frustration. She was an attractive, young mother who, at thirty-eight years old, had maintained her Coke-bottle figure. The jeans she wore hugged her curves, even after giving birth to her first son when she was only a teenager herself. Dré's nineteen year old brother, Savion, was away in the Air Force and was dearly missed by the entire family.

"Dré, do you have any idea how that sounds inside the house? What's wrong?" she asked as she sat down next to him.

Without making eye contact with her, he mumbled, "What's right, Momma?"

She touched his shoulder lovingly and whispered, "Dré."

"No, Momma. My life is a joke right now. I can't do anything I want to do. I might as well be dead."

"Don't say that, son. I know things are tough on you right now, but if you could hang in there just a little longer . . ."

Dré stood and yelled, "I'm tired of hanging in there! I know you hate this situation as much as I do. I don't know why you even stay with him."

She slid off the rock wall and got in her son's face as best she could. Dana was only five feet five inches tall, but she never acted like it. She was still able to stand toe to toe with Dré's six foot three frame.

"Don't you ever talk about your father like that, and watch your tone with me," she yelled back at him.

"I'm sorry, Momma."

Dana took a step back and said, "Son, I know this is hard, but sometimes you have to go through some unpleasant situations to get to what you really want in life. I want you to understand that I'm doing what we have to do. We have to trust the people who are in control of our lives right now and pray that in the end, we can get back to normal."

Still angry, Dré dropped the basketball on the ground and said, "I hope you're right, because I want my life back so I can play basketball again. I want to be able to see Denim and all my other friends without having to look over my shoulders every second of every day."

Dana caressed her son's cheek and said softly, "I know, and I'm so sorry."

Dré turned away from his mother. "It's not your fault. It's your husband's fault!"

She put her hands on her hips. "What did I tell just you?"

"Whatever," he replied sarcastically. His heart ached, being held hostage because of his father's business.

"Your father is finally doing something good for a change."

"Maybe so, but it's all at my expense!" he yelled. "What about my life? Don't I deserve a life too?"

She cupped his face and said, "Of course you do,

and as soon as Agent Miller tells us it's safe, things can get back to normal."

He put his arm around his mother's shoulders and said, "Momma, I hate to be the one to break this to you, but the life we knew before is gone. Do you think you'll ever feel safe again, regardless of what the Feds tell you?"

Dana hesitated and then said softly, "Yes, baby, I'm confident that they will get this matter taken care of so we can get back to our lives and you can be a normal teenager again."

"Nothing would make me happier. Playing basketball and going out with Denim is what I want the most. The coaches at school are really sweating me about joining the team. At this point, I don't even feel like working on my art anymore."

Dana thought for a second and then said, "You know what? Join the basketball team."

"Are you serious?"

"Yes, I'm serious." Dana wanted her son to be happy. Nothing was more important to her. She'd read where kids who felt sad or helpless often committed suicide, and the parents didn't have a clue. She didn't want her son to become a statistic.

"What are you going to tell your old man and Agent Miller?" he asked with concern.

She took a few steps toward the door and smiled. "Let me worry about them. There hasn't been a man yet that I couldn't handle. You're my son and I love you, and that's all I care about."

Dré lifted his mother off the ground and gave her a huge hug. She'd always been his ally and protected him. Now it appeared that she was going to go against his father, something she hadn't done in a while. The situation they were in was scary, dangerous, and indefinite, and it was because Dré's father had made numerous decisions to take risks with his family, all for the sake of making a quick buck. Now it was going to take a miracle to regain their lives or save them.

"Does this mean I can start seeing Denim again?"

"I know you miss Denim, but let's just handle one thing at a time. The distance between you two is probably good. I was beginning to worry that you might've been spending too much time together, if you know what I mean."

Dré laughed and walked across the driveway to pick up his basketball.

"You don't have to worry. I'm extra careful with Denim."

She eyed her son curiously. "If you're talking

about what I think you're talking about, that means you're treading in some dangerous territory."

"Momma!"

"Don't *Momma* me," she said as she pointed at him. "Just make sure you always—and I mean always—use protection. I'm too young to be a grandmother, so don't mess up."

Embarrassed, Dré blushed and said, "I know. Dang!"

Dana was serious about what she was saying to Dré. A lot of parents didn't talk to their sons like they did to their daughters when it came to sex. Making her position clear with him expelled any confusion or misunderstanding if an unplanned pregnancy were to arise.

"I won't mess up. I just hope she don't leave me over all of this stuff."

"If Denim cares about you like I think she does, she's not going anywhere," she answered as she touched his chin. "You're too charming."

"I don't know. It wasn't cool the way I left her."

Dana approached her son, who was still dribbling the basketball. She stole the ball from him and tucked it under her arm. "You didn't have a choice but to leave. Besides, I know you've been sneaking back into town to see Denim," she revealed as she handed him the basketball.

"What?"

"You heard me."

"Momma, honestly, today was the first time I saw Denim in a long time. I couldn't take it anymore. I had to see her," he admitted.

"You are so gullible. I was just teasing you about going back into town. I didn't know it was true. You didn't tell her anything, did you?" his mother asked.

He lowered his head. "No, ma'am."

Dana took her son's hand into hers. "You do know that she could really get hurt if someone thinks she knows where you live, don't you?"

"I wouldn't let that happen."

"How can you protect Denim if you're here and she's there?"

Frustrated, he said, "I don't know, I just can."

Dana opened the back door and stepped inside the house. Before closing the door, she said, "I don't have to remind you that the less she knows the better. Now, come on in so you can wash your hands for dinner."

Dré dribbled the basketball and threw one more

shot up at the goal before following his mother into the house. As expected, he hit a three-point shot, all net.

Inside the house, Dana and Dré found Garrett Patterson coming in from work. Dana greeted him with a kiss and asked, "How was your day?"

Garrett set his lunchbox on the kitchen countertop and mumbled, "Just another day on the assembly line."

"Well, dinner is ready, so go on up and get your shower so you can eat while it's hot."

Garrett acknowledged Dana by nodding as he walked over to the refrigerator and pulled out a cold bottle of beer. He opened it and took a sip as he stood there watching Dré set the table. Dana removed a bubbling chicken and cheese dish from the oven and set it on top of the oven.

Garrett took another sip of beer and then said, "Dré, you sure are quiet. Is there anything you want to talk about?"

While putting the last of the utensils on the table, he answered, "No, sir."

"Are you sure?" he asked as he turned up the bottle and drained the rest of the beer.

Dré finally made eye contact with his father as he walked past him. "I said no, sir."

Garrett grabbed Dré by the arm and pulled him against his chest. "Why do you have to give me attitude all the time?"

Dré looked into his father's eyes and said, "I'm not giving you attitude."

"You could've fooled me," Garrett replied as he released Dré's arm. "I heard you've been going back into town. I thought you were told not to leave this area or have contact with any of your friends."

Dré looked at his mother in disbelief. He had no idea how his father knew he'd been back to their hometown.

"Don't even stand there and try to think up a lie. There's not much you can get past me. You were told to stay away, and I expect you to follow my rules and those of Agent Miller."

"I had to see my friends!" he yelled. "I'm sick of being isolated down here!"

Garrett folded his arms and yelled, "Too bad! Make new friends!"

"I shouldn't have to!'

Dana stood frozen as she watched her husband and son yell at each other.

"Oh, but you're willing to get them killed?"

"Of course not, but they're still my friends, and I miss them."

Garrett thought for a moment. He knew he needed to calm down. It had been a stressful day at work, and ending it by yelling at his son was not something he'd planned to do.

"Dré, don't you realize that people know who your friends are? All they have to do is follow one of them, and then what do you think is going to happen? You're going to mess around and get all of us killed, including them. Where's your brain, son?"

Dré sat down at the table and put his head in his hands. "I've been careful, and I always make sure no one follows me."

Garrett burst out laughing. "It don't matter, Dré. People still know they're your friends. If you're meeting up with them, and the people we're being protected from decide to see what they know, what you think they're going to do to them?"

Silence engulfed the room for seconds; however, it seemed like hours.

Garrett finally broke the silence. "You're a good kid, Dré, and I know I haven't been the best father to you over the years, but I'm trying to do better. I promise when all of this is over, things will be different. I love you, son, and the last thing I want on my conscience is the death of my family or your friends. That's why I'm so hard on you."

Dana could see how broken her son was. She could also see that Garrett really did care about his family. Keeping the peace was her job, and reiterating what her husband said to Dré was very important at this moment.

"Dré, you have to understand what your father is saying. One mistake and it's all over. You don't get a second chance. This is not a situation any of us can take lightly."

"I know, Momma, but it seems like I'm the one getting lost in all of this. I've given up my whole life, and all I want to do is play basketball and see my friends. I don't think that's asking for too much."

Garrett put his hand on Dré's shoulder and said, "It is when you're talking about living or dying."

"Then let me play basketball. I need to have something in my life to keep me from going crazy." Dré had been a star basketball player before they were forced into hiding, and not only did he miss the game, the game missed him.

"You can't play ball right now. It's not safe, and

your talent will draw attention to you and to us. Just do what I say and stay away from your friends."

Dré looked his father in the eyes and pleaded with him. "I'm only asking for one thing, Daddy."

Garrett thought for a moment about his son's request and said, "Let me sleep on it," as he walked out of the kitchen and up the stairs.

Dré picked up his car keys and kissed his mother. "I'll be back in a second."

"Where are you going?"

"I don't know . . . to the store, anywhere; I just have to get out of here for a while."

"Well, while you're out, pick up a pie or something. I'm craving something sweet."

Dré nodded and quickly exited the kitchen.

Once he had pulled out of the driveway, Dana stormed upstairs to confront Garrett. She found him still in the shower, so she swung open the shower door and yelled, "I want my son to be happy, Garrett. I don't care what it takes, but make it happen. Dré needs to be able to play basketball, so do whatever you have to do to convince Agent Miller. If you can't, I have no problem taking Dré and moving to Atlanta or anywhere to start a new life without you!"

Garrett grabbed a towel and stepped out of the shower. "Are you serious?"

"You bet I'm serious," she replied as she backed away from him. "Dré is seventeen years old and he needs to live like a normal seventeen-year-old is supposed to live."

Garrett felt like the walls were closing in on him, and he knew a change would have to come soon if he wanted to keep his family together. Dana had never threatened to leave him before, so for her to mention it now, he knew she was serious.

Dré drove around town for about fifteen minutes before pulling into the supermarket parking lot. He made his way over to the bakery to look for a pie. He was torn between pecan pie and apple pie.

As he held the two pies in his hands, a man dressed casually in jeans and a golf shirt approached him and, with a smile, asked, "Don't I know you from somewhere?"

Startled, Dré set both pies down and said, "No, sir, you must have me confused with someone else."

The man followed Dré down the aisle as he tried to walk away from the stranger. "No, I never forget a face or a great athlete. You're André Patterson, the kid from Langley High School."

That's when it hit Dré. He'd been recognized by a perfect stranger, and he was stunned.

"I knew it was you. What happened to you? You were breaking all kinds of records and then you just disappeared. Did you get injured or something?"

Dré started sweating. He knew that he had to keep his composure and not give away his nervousness. He chuckled and said, "Something like that, sir, and then we moved."

"I'm sorry to hear that. I hope it's not a career-ending injury," the stranger stated with concern. "After you left, your basketball team went downhill, and they haven't recovered yet. You carried that team when you were there."

Dré looked at his watch and said, "I really have to go."

"It was nice seeing you again. I hope you get well soon," the stranger yelled out as he watched Dré turn the corner and disappear out of sight.

Dré hurried to his car and quickly drove off. As he drove down the street, he looked in his rearview mirror to make sure he wasn't being followed.

Minutes later, he pulled into the driveway and shut off the engine. Before exiting the car, he laid his head against the steering wheel and let out a breath. The encounter with the stranger shook him up, mostly because he had no idea who the man was. That man could spread the word all over town about where Dré lived.

When he entered the house, Dana noticed that his hands were empty and he looked ill. "Are you okay? Where's the pie?"

Dré set his keys on the countertop and said, "I didn't get a chance to buy it. I ran into a man in the store who recognized me from playing ball."

Dana dropped the glass she was holding in her hand, causing it to shatter on the tile floor.

Garrett stepped into the kitchen. "What's wrong?"

Dana couldn't speak. Garrett helped her over to a chair and then retrieved the broom and dust pan out of the closet.

"Dré, what's going on? What's wrong with your mother?"

"Some guy recognized me at the grocery store. He remembered me playing at Langley."

"See, that is exactly what I was afraid of! Who was he?" Garrett asked.

"I don't know," Dré replied as he caressed his mother's shoulders to comfort her.

Garrett swept up the broken glass and dumped it into the garbage can. "Get your mother some water."

Dré opened the refrigerator and pulled out a bottle of water and handed it to his mother.

Garrett sat down next to Dana and took her hand into his. "I thought with us living a hundred miles away from the area it would be far enough for us to be safe. I'll have to call Agent Miller and let them know what happened. We might have to move again."

"No!" Dana hit her fist on the table. "I want this to be over! That's the only thing that you need to talk to the Feds about. I'm with Dré now. I want my life back! I miss my parents and my friends, and I hate not being able to see them. I'm not moving again."

"I need you to hang in there with me a little longer," he pleaded.

"No, Garrett. I've stood beside you and supported you through all your dirt. Now it's time for you to support me and our son."

"I didn't know it was going to be like this. I'm sorry I got you two involved in this."

Dana and Dré stared at Garrett, who, for the first time, seemed broken.

"Garrett, you have to understand that we're trapped in this with you. You made the decision to testify against those awful people without thinking about what it was going to do to our lives."

He covered his face with his hands and then looked up and yelled, "Would it have been better if I had kept my mouth shut and gone to jail?"

"That's not what I'm saying," Dana yelled back at him. "You're my husband and I love you, but Dré needs a life. It just seems like there could've been other options."

"Maybe so, but all I know is that at the time, I was jammed up and the Feds offered me a way out and I took it."

No one said anything for a few seconds. Garrett eventually broke the silence and said softly, "Let's eat. We'll talk more about it later."

Dana and Dré took their seats at the table, where they joined hands and Garrett blessed the food. He asked God for strength and guidance, and prayed for the safety of his family.

Chapter Five

A couple of weeks had passed since Denim met Dré at the lake. She still couldn't stop thinking about the anonymous text message she believed to have been sent by Dré. All it said was JOHN 15:9. Denim wasn't familiar with the scripture, so after she received it, she had quickly grabbed her Bible to look it up.

As the Father loved Me, I also have loved you; abide in My love.

She had memorized the scripture, and any time she felt discouraged or lonely, she recited it.

It was now the day before Denim's first day on her new job, and she was really looking forward to it. Most of her classmates had jobs, and those who didn't, wished they did, unless they were on the lazy side. Her hometown was just the right size. It wasn't too small, so it had plenty to do to keep teens entertained, but it wasn't too big to keep them from losing their freedom due to high crime statistics.

On this particular day, she was shopping for new scrubs to wear to work. Denim loved working, but she mostly enjoyed making her own money. This meant freedom to buy her own clothes, go out to eat with friends, and keep gas in her prized possession, her father's restored Mustang.

As she scanned through the racks of scrubs, she found several that she liked. The ones she favored the most were decorated with cartoon characters like Sponge Bob Square Pants, Tinker Bell, and other Disney and Nickelodeon characters. Denim purchased a set of five. Now all she had to do was purchase some fresh athletic shoes. After a brief search, she found the shoes she was interested in buying. One set was a pair of black New Balance shoes, the other a pair of white Nike, and lastly, a pair of red-and-white Reeboks.

The young salesman who assisted her couldn't take his eyes off her. It was a wonder he was able to give her the correct shoes to try on, especially since the designer jeans and Rocawear T-shirt she wore showed off all her shapely curves. He appeared to be in his late twenties, and in reality, she was too young for him. Besides, it wasn't like she wanted to date him, though she did appreciate the attention.

Denim thanked the young salesman as he gathered all three boxes of shoes and took them over to the cash register to ring up her purchases. As she walked toward the checkout counter, she was nearly knocked down by a very pregnant Patrice.

The chance meeting caught both of them off guard. Neither knew what to say or how to react. As they stood there face to face, Denim couldn't help but glance down at Patrice's enormous belly. By her calculations, she had to be at least seven months pregnant. It had been months since Denim had seen Patrice, especially since she no longer attended their high school. Patrice's mother, a college professor, now homeschooled her so she could keep up with her classmates.

As Denim stared at Patrice, she could see a subtle glow radiating from her face. It was a glow she often heard people talk about in regards to pregnant women, and the fuchsia top she wore with a pair of black Capri pants enhanced the glow. It was obvious that Patrice was just as shocked as Denim was to run into her old friend; however, Denim didn't want to give Patrice the satisfaction of knowing she was a little shaken to see her.

"What's up?" Denim asked sarcastically.

Patrice caressed her stomach and said, "I guess you can see what's up with me. What about you?"

"Nothing except school and work."

"I see," Patrice responded awkwardly.

"Yeah."

"Where are you working?" Patrice asked.

Denim watched shoppers as they wandered in and out of the store. She cleared her throat and said, "I just got a job at that new physical therapy clinic downtown, across the street from the hospital."

Patrice nodded and said, "Oh, I've seen that building. You like it?"

A faint smile appeared on Denim's face. "I don't know yet. I start tomorrow."

"Oh! So I guess physical therapy is your thang, huh?" Patrice asked.

"It appears that way," Denim admitted as she looked at her watch and stepped around Patrice. "Well, I have to go. Take care of yourself and your baby."

As Denim walked away, Patrice called out to her, "Denim!"

She turned and walked back over to her. "Yes?"

Patrice hesitated briefly. She opened her mouth to say something, but the words wouldn't come out. She wanted their friendship to be like it used to be, but she didn't want to make a fool of herself either.

"Do you have something you want to say to me, Patrice?"

Stuttering, Patrice responded by saying, "Well, uh, yeah, uh, DeMario told me he hung out with you and Dré the other day."

"Yeah. What about it?"

Patrice shrugged her shoulders. "I don't know. Do you know what's going on with Dré?"

Denim laughed out loud. "What makes you think I know? DeMario's your man. I'm sure he tells you everything."

Denim's response hurt her feelings. This was hard for her, and Denim wasn't making it any easier. "I just figured since you guys were hanging out, you knew."

"Well, you figured wrong."

"You don't have to be so mean. I know we're not like we used to be, but damn!"

"Listen, Patrice, I'm not trying to be mean, but it's kind of weird running into you after all this time. I sort of don't know what to say to you or how to feel."

Tears welled up in Patrice's eyes. "Have you ever thought about apologizing to me?"

Denim frowned and put her hand on her hip. "Apologize?"

Patrice held her hand up and said, "Never mind. I figured it would be too much for you to do."

"Whatever!" Denim replied as she turned to walk away again.

Patrice grabbed Denim's arm and said softly, "I'm not your enemy. I miss you. Don't you miss me at all?"

Denim looked down at Patrice's hand on her arm and then up into her eyes. "Let go of my arm, Patrice."

Patrice removed her hand and asked, "Why do you hate me so much?"

Denim walked over to the register without responding and pulled out her debit card. As she waited for the salesman to ring up her purchases, Patrice walked over and stood next to her.

"Why can't you answer my question?"

Denim handed her debit card to the salesman

and turned to Patrice. "Because I don't want to. Now, leave it alone."

The salesman eyed the two women as he bagged Denim's purchases. As they carried on their tense conversation, the salesman noticed that it was starting to get a little more heated. He interrupted them by asking Patrice if she wanted to try on any shoes.

Patrice smiled and said, "No, thank you. I was just looking around."

Denim grabbed her bag and thanked the salesman. She hurried toward the exit. Just as Patrice took a step to follow her, a sharp pain hit her lower region, causing her to cry out in pain.

Denim turned to find Patrice doubled over in pain. She didn't know if Patrice was playing a trick on her to get her to stay, or if she was really in pain.

"That's a foul way to get my attention, Patrice."

"I'm not joking, Denim."

Denim walked back over to Patrice and then helped her over to a chair. "Are you okay?"

Moaning, Patrice said, "I don't know. All I know is it hurts."

Denim pulled out her cell phone and said, "I

can't do this. You need to get to the hospital. I'm calling paramedics and I'm calling DeMario."

"Wait!" Patrice yelled. "I can't do this by myself."

Agitated, she said, "This is not my responsibility! I'm calling DeMario."

The salesman walked over to them and asked, "Is everything okay?"

"No!" Denim yelled as she looked down at Patrice. "Can't you see she's in labor?"

The salesman looked down at Patrice and noticed that she was in agony. "I'm calling paramedics," he replied.

"No! Please, I'll be fine," Patrice replied right before another sharp pain hit her.

Denim looked at the salesman and then back at Patrice.

"What do you want me to do?" the salesman asked.

Denim dropped her cell phone into her purse and then said, "Don't call the paramedics. I'm going to take her to the hospital myself. Patrice, do you think you can make it out to the parking lot?"

"I think so," Patrice replied as the salesman helped her out of the chair.

Denim reached inside her pocket and pulled out her car keys. "Thanks for all your help."

He looked at Denim and smiled. "Go ahead and pull your car around to the mall's entrance around the corner, and I'll help your friend outside."

"Thank you," Denim replied, then hurried out the door and into the parking lot to retrieve her car.

Minutes later, Denim pulled up to the curb to pick up Patrice. The young salesman opened the passenger's side door and helped Patrice into the car.

"Thank you so much for your help," Denim called out to the salesman as she buckled Patrice's seatbelt. She made a mental note of the name shown on his nametag.

"You're welcome," he replied. "I hope everything turns out okay."

Denim waved as she pulled away from the curb. She looked over at Patrice, who had a stressful expression on her face. "How are you doing?"

"Not good. I just had another pain," she revealed.

Denim pulled into traffic and nervously asked, "Do you think you're really in labor?"

"I don't know. It's too early. Oh God, I can't lose my baby."

"You're not going to lose your baby, Patrice. Just calm down."

Patrice was breathing in and out loudly to try to ease her pain.

"Just how far along are you?" Denim asked anxiously.

With a grimace on her face, she said, "About seven months."

"DeMario needs to know what's going on. He should be here with you, not me."

"I know you can't wait to get rid of me, Denim, so when we get to the hospital, you can drop me off and do what you do best—disappear."

Denim frowned. "Stop bitching! You just make sure your water don't break in my car."

"Ouch!" the young mother to be yelled out, causing Denim to swerve out of her lane of traffic.

"What?" Denim screamed. "Did your water break?"

"No, I had another pain, but this one was stronger. Hurry, Denim."

Denim grabbed her cell phone . "I don't care what you say. I'm calling DeMario whether you like it or not."

Patrice closed her eyes and laid her head against the headrest. She was in too much pain to argue about it. Denim and the baby were in control now.

Denim dialed frantically and waited for DeMario to answer.

"Hey, DeMario, it's Denim. I need you to meet me at the hospital. I have your girl in my car and I think she's in labor."

"What? How? Is she okay?"

"All I know is she's in a lot of pain. Just meet us at the hospital."

"I'm on my way. And whatever you do, take care of my girl and my baby," he requested before hanging up and hurrying out the door.

Chapter Six

Hours later, DeMario wheeled Patrice out of the hospital with Denim following close behind.

Standing on the sidewalk, Denim clapped her hands together and said, "Well, guys, I'm glad that's over. I guess false labor can be a hassle, huh?"

"Yeah," DeMario replied. "Thanks for hanging out."

"No problem. Well, I have to get going. Tomorrow's my first day at work, and I have to stop and get gas before I head home."

DeMario put the brake down on the wheelchair and hugged her. "Thanks for everything, sis."

"You're welcome, bro."

DeMario pulled his keys out of his pocket and twirled them on his finger. "Do you mind waiting here with Patrice while I get the car?"

She looked at the time on her cell phone and said, "Yeah, but hurry up, DeMario."

"I'm hurrying," he yelled back as he ran across the parking lot.

Denim and Patrice watched in silence as DeMario ran to his car. Denim sat down on a nearby bench to wait. Patrice released the brake on the wheelchair and maneuvered it over to her former best friend. She stopped directly in front of her and just stared at her face.

"You really do hate me, don't you?"

"I don't hate you, Patrice," she mumbled as she fumbled with her cell phone.

"Then why can't you look at me?"

"I don't want to talk about it right now."

"You don't want to talk about anything anymore. We used to be so close."

"Well, people change."

Tears welled up in Patrice's eyes. "I haven't changed, but I see that you have. Your heart is so cold. You used to smile and light up the room, but not anymore."

Denim stood when she saw DeMario approaching in the car. "I'm not cold. I'm hurt, and I just hope that one day you'll understand why I feel the way I do."

"Maybe you're right, but for what it's worth, thanks for being there for me today and getting me to the hospital."

"You're welcome," Denim replied as she pulled her purse up on her shoulder.

DeMario pulled up to the curb and exited the vehicle. "Are you ready to go, babe?"

"I'll see you later," Denim said. "Good luck with everything, and drive safely."

DeMario smiled and said, "Gracias, my sister. Shoot me a text when you get home."

She threw up her hand and said, "Will do."

Patrice watched in silence as Denim walked across the parking lot to her car.

DeMario turned back to Patrice and asked, "Did you and Denim get into an argument or something?"

Patrice inched her way out of the wheelchair and into the car with DeMario's assistance. "I'm through talking about Denim. I'm tired and I want to go to bed."

"I know, babe. I'll get you home in just a second, but I need to holler at Denim before she pulls off."

Before Patrice could protest, DeMario was already jogging across the asphalt.

"Denim! Wait a second!"

She rolled down her window. "Did you forget something?"

"Yeah, I wanted to talk to you for a second."

"What about?"

DeMario looked over at Patrice sitting in the car, and then back at his friend. "I don't know what went down between you and Patrice today, but you need to know that she's really fragile right now with the baby and all, and she could really use a friend."

Denim put her hand up to stop him before he went any further. "Don't force this on me, De-Mario."

"Come on, you can do better than that. I didn't want to say anything in front of her, but the doctor said she's really going to have to be careful these next few weeks."

"Why?" Denim asked.

DeMario sighed. "Her blood pressure is up, and the doctors said she's retaining fluid in her feet and hands. They're worried about it going into toxemia."

"What's toxemia?"

"The way they explained it was that it's high blood pressure brought on by the pregnancy. If

Patrice doesn't watch it, they'll put her on bed rest."

She turned on the car's ignition and said, "I'm sorry. I hope Patrice and the baby are okay."

"I'm worried. This toxemia could kill her and the baby."

"Are you serious?"

"You know I wouldn't joke about this. Patrice is really going to need a friend to get through this until she has the baby."

Denim was concerned about Patrice and the baby, but this was too much for her to take in right now. "Go home and get some rest. I'm sure Patrice and the baby will be okay."

He backed away from her car and said, "I hope you're right. I'll see you tomorrow."

"You will?" she asked curiously.

"Yeah. I told my dad I wanted to move back in with my mom, so I transferred back to Langley."

"That's so cool. I guess that means I'll get to see you every day."

"Most definitely. Drive carefully, Denim."

"You too."

On the way home, Denim thought about her conversations with Patrice and DeMario. She missed them both, and wanted to let go of her anger toward Patrice for getting pregnant. Their plans were already set to go off to college together and be roommates, but with a baby on the way, there was no way that could happen now.

As Denim drove through town, she thought about how unimportant her feud with Patrice was starting to become to her. Two lives were at stake, and she definitely didn't want anything bad to happen to Patrice or her baby.

Denim looked down at her gas meter. At the next block, she pulled into a gas station to fill up her car. While there, she decided to go inside to get a Pepsi and a bag of Doritos. Within minutes, she had her drink and chips in hand and made her way up the aisle.

Just as she set the items on the counter, two men burst through the doors with handguns. One immediately shot out the surveillance camera, while the other one ordered the clerk to open the register. Denim trembled uncontrollably once she realized she was in the middle of an armed robbery.

As one gunman yelled at the clerk to put all the money in a bag, the other one ordered Denim to hand over her purse.

"Hey, slim, what you got?" the guy yelled as he yanked her purse out of her hand.

"All I have is this twenty." She held up the money in her hand.

The gunman snatched the twenty-dollar bill out of her hand and started to open her purse when the first gunman eyed Denim, taking a closer look at her.

"What's your name, shorty?"

"D-D-Denim," she replied nervously.

The gunman looked at his accomplice and said, "Damn! Give her back her stuff, man. She's cool."

"What the hell are you talking about? This purse has to be worth at least fifty on the streets, and that car outside . . .

"I said give her back her damn money!" he yelled. "That's Li'l Carl's girl. Now, hurry up! We gotta go!"

Denim heard what he said, but she couldn't believe her ears. She wasn't Li'l Carl's girl, though she had been his friend.

The second gunman looked at Denim and laughed. "I'll be damned! It is her." He gave Denim her money and the purse. "Sorry, slim. Get out of here. We have some business to conduct."

Denim noticed her hands were trembling as she held them out to retrieve her purse.

"Thank you," she whispered as she stared at the frightened clerk.

She couldn't believe that knowing Carlton had saved her from harm, but she knew it might not be enough to save the clerk. She decided to step out on faith.

"You know, you guys don't have to do this. If money is what you want, I can help you get a job."

The two men burst out laughing. "You're talking crazy. This is our job. Hurry up with the money, man!" he yelled when he looked over at the clerk.

Denim walked closer to the taller one and pleaded with him. "Please don't hurt this man. I'm sure he has a family, and if you hurt him, you won't only be messing up his family's lives, but yours as well."

The two men burst out laughing again. The other one asked, "What makes you think we're going to hurt him?"

"I can see it in your eyes. Listen, I'll give you my money, my purse, and my car, but don't hurt him."

The clerk stood frozen in his spot, still holding the bag of money. The other gunman grabbed the bag of money and then pointed his gun at the clerk and smiled.

"Today is your lucky day. You'd better be glad sweet little Denim was here tonight. She just saved your life."

Before leaving, they fired off a shot over the clerk's head. Then, with the blink of an eye, they were gone, leaving Denim and the clerk alone.

"Are you okay?" she asked softly.

The clerk sank to the floor and began to sob.

Denim hugged him and said, "They're gone and you're safe."

She picked up the store telephone and called the police. Within a couple of minutes, the store was surrounded squad cars.

As they questioned Denim, she explained to the police that she didn't know who the men were and that they knew her through her association with Carlton. The clerk corroborated Denim's story and credited her for saving his life. Once the police were satisfied that Denim was not an accomplice, they followed her home so they could explain things to her parents.

Samuel Mitchell opened the door and found Denim standing on the porch next to a police officer. "What the . . ."

The officer held his hand up to calm Samuel. "It's

okay, Mr. Mitchell. I'm here with your daughter on a good note. May I come in?"

Samuel stepped aside and allowed them to enter. He closed the door and looked over at Denim. "What's going on? Are you okay?"

"I'm fine, Daddy," she answered as she set her purse on the hallway table.

Samuel escorted the officer into the family room and asked, "What is this about, officer?"

"Well, sir, your daughter is somewhat of a hero. She saved a man's life tonight. You and your wife have reason to be very proud of her."

Samuel smiled and put his arm around Denim's shoulder. "What did you do, baby?"

"It was nothing, Daddy."

The officer smiled and said, "It was more than nothing. Two men robbed a convenience store where your daughter was buying gas. From what Denim tells us, one of them recognized her and decided to let her go."

Samuel looked over at Denim and asked, "Did you know these guys, honey?"

"No, Daddy. I'd never seen them before, but somehow they knew me because of my association with Carlton."

The police officer interrupted, saying, "Mr. Mitchell, Denim was at the right place at the right time. It was dangerous what she did, but she refused to leave the store clerk alone, and because of it, the clerk is going home to his family."

"Denim, this could've turned out so differently."

"I know, Daddy, but once I knew they weren't going to hurt me, I couldn't leave that man in there to die."

"She's right, Mr. Mitchell. After she convinced those thugs to just take the money and leave, they left without anyone getting harmed."

Tears welled up in Samuel's eyes. "You took a big risk, but I'm proud of you."

The officer stood and took a step toward the door. "I wish there were more adults like Denim . . . and she's a teenager."

"So do I, officer. I appreciate everything that you've done for my daughter."

"That's my job, sir. Have a good night. And Denim, keep up the good work. Have a great night."

Samuel and Denim walked the officer to the door. "Thank you, officer."

"You're welcome. . . . Oh! Before I go, I need to tell you that Denim and a few other citizens are going to be recognized by the Mayor for their out-standing contribution to the community. We'll contact you soon and let you know the date of the ceremony."

Denim smiled. "Thank you."

"Yes, thank you, officer. Denim's mother is at church right now, but I can't wait to tell her what happened."

"Give her my regards. Good night."

Denim and Samuel waved at the officer as he drove away.

"Daddy, I'm going to bed. It's been a long night. Give Momma a kiss for me when she gets home, okay?"

Samuel kissed her forehead and said, "I will. Sleep well, and again, I'm so proud of you, sweetheart."

Upstairs, Denim quickly took her shower and then lay across the bed. As she lay there, she stared up at the ceiling and thought about the events of the day. First she had the drama with Patrice, and now the robbery. It was a lot to absorb for one day, and she felt like she was about to jump out of her skin.

She rolled over on her stomach, opened her nightstand, and pulled out her denim diary. She thought about what she was going to write. Minutes later, the words flowed out of her, and she began to write about her experience:

Dear Diary,

I don't know where to begin tonight, since so much happened today. I ran into Patrice and her big old belly at the mall. I could tell she felt awkward, and she should have. Me? I'm still pissed. Can you believe she tried to hold a conversation with me without trying to apologize?

The next thing I knew, she started screaming out in pain. There I was, stuck, as she started talking about being in labor. It wasn't my fault that she got herself pregnant, so I told the sales clerk to call her an ambulance. When Patrice heard that, she freaked out and started begging me not to leave her. There I was, stuck in a shoe store with a crazy pregnant girl.

I don't mean to be coldhearted; I just have a hard time with forgiveness. I know it's not the Christian way to be, but I'm sorry. I'm just going to have to pray about it.

Anyway, I took that knucklehead to the

hospital, but they sent her home because it was false labor.

Then to top things off, on my way home I stopped for gas and walked in on a robbery by some of Li'l Carl's crew. They were going to rob me too, but once they recognized me, they let me go. Fortunately, I was able to talk them out of hurting the clerk because if I hadn't been there, those fools would've busted a cap in him for sure.

I now feel like I've become a human magnet for drama. Lord, help me! God, I miss Dré!

Later,
D

Chapter Seven

The next morning, Denim woke up and found her father in the family room eating a bowl of fruit and watching a football game he'd taped two nights earlier.

"Good morning, Daddy," she greeted him as she picked up a bagel and popped it in the toaster.

Samuel turned the volume down on the TV. "Good Morning."

Denim waited for the bagel to finish toasting. "Where's Momma?"

"She got a call and had to go into work early."

"I was hoping to talk to her before I left for school."

"Give her a call on the way. I know she's anxious to talk to you too."

"Okay," she answered as she took a bite of her bagel.

Denim sat next to her father and watched the football game as she ate. She was a huge football fan as well, and along with her brother, Antoine, grew up watching football games by her father's side. Samuel's work schedule sometimes caused him to miss some of his favorite games, and he did his best to steer clear of the outcome before having a chance to watch it on TiVo.

"What's going on with Patrice? Your mother told me she had a scare with the pregnancy yesterday."

"I don't know, Daddy. You know Patrice and I are not friends anymore."

Samuel tilted his head and looked over at Denim. "What do you mean you don't know? Didn't you take her to the hospital?"

She fidgeted in her seat as she finished off her bagel.

"Yes, sir, but it was by accident. I just happened to run into her at the mall and she started having pains."

He shook his head and said, "I don't know what happened between you two, but I'm sure whatever it is, it can be resolved."

"I doubt it," she softly replied. "DeMario told me that she could get something called toxemia."

He set his coffee cup in the sink and said, "Oh man, that's bad news."

"Really?"

Samuel turned the TV off and turned to his daughter. "Go see your friend and salvage what you can of your friendship. Patrice needs you now more than ever. If that toxemia builds up in her, she could die, and I know you don't want that to happen before you make things right between you."

"Of course not, but things have gone so far. I wouldn't blame Patrice if she never speaks to me again."

Denim thought about how she had treated Patrice the day before, when it was obvious that Patrice was trying to make amends with her. Even then she didn't want to give in, because she was still hurt and disappointed that their pact had been broken by the unplanned pregnancy.

Samuel stroked his daughter's cheek. "She might make you eat a little crow at first, but I'm sure in time, she'll come around and you girls will be upstairs giggling like you used to."

Denim grabbed her book bag and said, "If you say so. I'd better get going."

Samuel looked at his watch and said, "I need to get going myself. Have a great day at school."

"I will," she replied as she kissed his cheek and hurried out the door.

As soon as Denim walked into school, she noticed that she was getting a lot more attention than normal. Her classmates were whispering and pointing at her as she made her way down the hallway to her locker. While she was turning the combination on her locker, DeMario leaned up against the locker next to hers and frowned. Denim looked over at him and smiled.

"Hey, stranger. Welcome back to Langley."

"Thanks, Denim. Listen, I know it's my first day back, but I'm hearing some stuff about you that I don't like."

"Excuse me?" she answered, startled by DeMario's remark.

"Don't excuse me. Word on the street is that Li'l Carl's crew has labeled you hands off, which usually means you're a part of their crew."

Denim's eyes widened as she closed her locker. "What are you talking about?"

"I didn't stutter. I heard it from a very reliable source that you're hands off. Now, tell me what's going on," he asked with his voice slightly elevated. This caused people to stare in their direction, embarrassing her.

"Chill, DeMario."

"No, I will not chill!" he announced with anger. "Let me break this down for you, sis. The guy that took over Li'l Carl's crew after his murder said that Denim Mitchell is not to be messed with by anyone, or there would be hell to pay."

Denim shook her head in disbelief and said, "I don't know anything about me being hands off, but I did get mixed up in something last night after I left you guys. That's probably the reason you're hearing those lies."

Curious, he asked, "What happened?"

"When I stopped for gas on the corner of Fifth and Lincoln, two guys from Li'l Carl's crew burst in and started robbing the place. They were going to rob me, too, until one of them recognized me."

"What do you mean, recognized you?" DeMario asked.

"I don't know, DeMario. I guess Li'l Carl told them about me or something. I've never seen them before in my life, and they had bandanas over their faces."

He let out a breath and said, "Denim, you can't be associated with these guys. They're bad news, and they have rivals who wouldn't think twice about hurting you just to piss them off, especially if they think you're of any value to them."

"Do you honestly think this is something I asked for?"

"No, but because of your association with Li'l Carl, you've stepped right in the middle of one of the worst gangs in the hood."

"What do you think I should do?"

"I don't know. Give me time to think," he replied. "This is a mess. Dré is going to go ballistic when he hears about it."

She held her books close to her chest. "You don't have to tell me. I don't want this, DeMario!"

At that moment, the bell rang. DeMario nudged her said, "I know. Come on, we have to get to class."

The pair walked side by side down the hallway, where Denim continued to be the subject of whispers and stares. Occasionally, students would point at her and then move out of her way.

"Ignore them."

"I'm trying to ignore them. I just hope nobody tries to step to me like I'm really a part of Li'l Carl's crew."

Before the words were out of her mouth, a young man stepped out in front of them, stopping them in their tracks. DeMario quickly moved in front of Denim in her defense and asked, "What's up?"

The teen smiled, showing several gold teeth. "Nothing's up, bro. I'm here to talk to Denim. Besides, this has nothing to do with you."

"You might not think it has anything to do with me, but she's a friend of mine, so it involves me."

"That's cool," the young man said with a sly grin. "I can respect that."

DeMario looked the young man up and down and then said, "I've seen you around and I know who you hang with. Denim's not happy with the spotlight you guys have put on her. Y'all need to straighten that bull out."

The teenager put his hands up in defense and said, "Hold up, bro. I come in peace. It's all good."

DeMario folded his arms and firmly announced, "No, it's not all good, and I would highly suggest you put the word out that Denim's *not* a part of your crew before some of your rivals try to step to her."

Agitated, the teen asked, "Do you know who you're talking to? Denim has nothing to worry about. A person would have to be a fool to step to her."

Just as DeMario was about to respond, Denim grabbed his arm and interrupted him. "DeMario, I got this."

Somewhat hesitant, he stepped aside and allowed her to address the young man.

"What's your name?" she asked.

"Everybody knows I'm Boomerang. I just want you to know that Rock told me to look after you."

"I didn't ask for this and I don't want it," she announced. "And who is Rock?"

He leaned in and whispered, "I believe you met him last night."

Denim swallowed hard, realizing that Rock must've been one of the robbers.

"Listen, Boomerang, you tell Rock I'm cool the way I am and that I don't need anybody looking after me."

"I don't think Rock is going to like it that you're turning down his generous offer," he explained. "He's not a man that takes rejection easily."

"That's not my problem. And while you're at it, tell Rock that Li'l Carl was my friend, and even he didn't force himself or his lifestyle on me, so I don't expect Rock to either."

DeMario looked over at Denim. He was surprised by her boldness, but was glad she stood up to the teen. If she showed fear, the conversation might go in a different direction.

"I don't do gangs . . . period."

Boomerang laughed. "That's cool, but I'm only following orders."

"I'm not trying to be disrespectful to you or your crew, but being associated with a gang is not my thang."

"You're hard, but I like that in a woman. Li'l Carl and Rock was right about you. You are da bomb. I'll give him the message, but I can't say how he'll respond," he revealed as he backed away.

"Boomerang, before you go, I would appreciate it if you would apologize to DeMario and assure me that no one will mess with him in any way," Denim requested.

Boomerang looked at DeMario and without hesitation, he put his hand out and said, "My bad, Dee. If you're cool with Denim, I guess you're cool with the crew."

DeMario refused to shake Boomerang's hand. He didn't want to give their classmates any false impressions like they already had about Denim. The handshake might make them think he was a part of the crew.

He looked around at the crowd of kids congregating in the hallway and said discreetly, "Cool, but I'll pass on the handshake. I don't want people around here to get the wrong idea."

Boomerang nodded in agreement and slid his hands in his pockets. "That's cool."

"So, are we all good now?" Denim asked.

Boomerang nodded at the pair and said, "We're good. Later."

Denim and DeMario watched Boomerang as he disappeared in the crowded hallway.

After entering the classroom and taking their seats, DeMario put his head in his hands and asked, "Do you realize what you just did?"

"No, what?" she asked as she took out her notebook.

"I think the conversation with Boomerang was a mistake, especially in front of everyone."

"Why do say that?"

DeMario stuck a peppermint in his mouth. "I don't think they're going to go away like you think they are. You showed no fear in talking to that dude, and you challenged him. Damn, girl."

Denim swallowed the lump in her throat. From what DeMario was saying, she was right back where she started. Because she'd had the tense conversation with Boomerang in front of everyone, it all but confirmed she was part of the crew.

DeMario reached over and gave her hand a soft squeeze just as their teacher entered the classroom. She was his friend, and he knew he had to help her out of this situation one way or another.

Chapter Eight

For the rest of the day, Denim was continually subjected to pointing and staring from her classmates. At one point, she was approached in the restroom by four girls—Zeta, Deirdre, Jasmine, and Tyra—all who were known to be the girlfriends of members of Li'l Carl's crew.

"Are you Denim?" Zeta asked.

Denim washed her hands without looking at them. "Who wants to know?"

They laughed and then Tyra said, "Don't try to be cute. You already think you all that with your designer clothes and pimped-out car."

"I don't think anything," Denim replied as she reached for a paper towel and dried her hands.

"The crew said you were hands off. What makes

you so special?" Tyra asked. "You bet' not be messing with *my man*."

Denim rolled her eyes and said, "Please! I wouldn't have any of your men, whoever they might be."

"Oh! So now you do think you're better than us?" Jasmine asked.

"I don't think anything," Denim replied as she pushed past them. "Listen, just get out of my way and leave me alone."

"Chill, you guys," Deirdre requested. "Denim's a part of the crew now, so she deserves the same respect as the rest of us."

Denim turned and yelled, "I'm not a part of anything!"

When Denim tried to walk past them, Zeta and Jasmine blocked the door.

"You're going to stand here in our face and disrespect us after we came in here to try and show you some love? I don't think so," Zeta replied.

Denim's face instantly became hot when she realized she was in a sticky situation. She'd never had to fight, but there was a first time for everything.

"I'm not going to tell you again," Denim responded through gritted teeth. "Get out of my way!"

Zeta and Jasmine immediately grabbed Denim's arms and pushed her against the wall, causing her to hit her head. It was at that moment that a senior, known by the street name Patience, and her younger sister, Comonica, walked into the bathroom.

Patience was the head of a girls' gang who called themselves B.G.R., which stood for Brown Girls Rule. Patience stood all of five feet nine inches. She was a beautiful teenager, but had a glare that could melt ice. Her personality could be deceiving because she appeared to have a calmness about her; however, rumor had it that she wasn't one to cross. Her battle scars included one on her arm and another one on the side of her face. These scars represented the brutality of the life she led as a gangsta girl, but somehow it didn't take away from her natural beauty.

Comonica was a junior and second in command of the gang. She, too, was tall and attractive, but had a shorter fuse when it came to altercations. She was in charge of "jumping in" potential members of B.G.R. This meant that in order to join, they had to endure a beating by members of the gang to see how tough they were.

Patience looked at the situation and smiled. She folded her arms and calmly said, "I said let her go."

"Stay out of this, Patience. This has nothing to do with you or B.G.R."

Patience walked over to the girls, looked in the mirror, and ran her hand through her long, wavy hair. She then turned to the girls, and this time her request was firmer.

"I said let her go!"

Zeta stepped up to Patience and said, "You can't walk up in here and interfere with crew business. This has nothing to do with you."

Before Zeta got the last syllable out of her mouth, Patience had her against the mirror by the throat. The other girls immediately scattered, leaving Zeta alone with Patience.

Comonica started laughing, while Denim stood frozen in her tracks. She didn't understand why Patience came to her defense, but she was glad she had. They'd never crossed paths before, and Patience had never even acknowledged her existence. Why she was coming to her aid today was a mystery.

"You know what, Zeta? I hate bitches who don't listen. I asked you nicely the first time; now you've pissed me off. Mitchell is not a gangsta girl. Never has been and never will be, so stay out of her face. You got that?"

Zeta nodded as tears streamed down her face. Patience released her and said, "Now I think you owe her an apology."

Zeta coughed and rubbed her neck. "I'm sorry, Denim. I didn't mean to roll up on you like I did."

"Apology accepted," Denim whispered.

"Now get out of here," Patience ordered the young girl.

Zeta quickly exited the bathroom, leaving Denim, Patience, and Comonica alone.

"You cool?" Patience asked Denim as she looked at her through the reflection of the mirror.

Denim swallowed the lump in her throat and said, "Yes. Thank you."

Patience reached into her book bag and pulled out some lip gloss. After applying it, she said, "No problem. It's all in a day's work. Maybe one day you'll return the favor."

Seconds later, Denim found herself alone in the restroom and clueless about what had just happened. She was grateful to Patience, but hoped she never had to cross paths with her or the crew girls ever again.

* * *

After the welcome sound of the last period bell, Denim sat in her car in the student parking lot and pulled her diary out of her book bag and began to write.

Dear Diary,

Today was another crazy day. Because of what happened at the gas station, people now think I'm part of Li'l Carl's crew. For some reason, they've labeled me "hands off." Then, to top that off, some of those crew girls tried to confront me in the bathroom. I thought I was going to have to fight my way out until Patience and her sister Comonica came in and interrupted them. Patience defended me, which surprised me, since we've never had any dealings. I was happy, though, because it would've been tough for me to fight all four of the girls from the crew.

D

"Denim!"
She looked up from her diary and saw DeMario walking her way. She tucked her diary back into her book bag and climbed out of her car.

"Hey, DeMario. What's up?"

He greeted her with a hug and asked, "You tell me."

Denim leaned against the car and watched the coming and going of students. "Some girls from the crew cornered me in the restroom and tried to test me."

DeMario twirled his keys on his finger and said, "I'm not surprised. Hopefully it won't be like this tomorrow, and all the drama will have died down."

"I don't know, DeMario. If anything, I think it's going to get worse."

"What do you mean?" he asked.

"When those girls were confronting me in the bathroom, Patience walked in and nearly choked one of them to death."

DeMario burst out laughing. "You mean Patience the Amazon?"

"Yes! I nearly passed out. She made them leave me alone and then walked out like nothing ever happened."

"Damn," he replied. "Scary, huh?"

"You got that right. I thought Patience was going to kill Zeta. I never want to be in that situation again. You know I'm not the confrontational type, but I will throw down if I have to."

"I have no doubt."

The two friends continued to talk about the confrontation and past incidents involving teen gang members at their school. The Resource Officers did what they could to keep the students under control by patrolling the hallways. Unfortunately, some fights were over by the time they made their way through the crowded hallways, leaving them to decipher who the perpetrators were, since most students didn't snitch.

"How's Patrice?" she asked to change the subject.

"She's fine, just grouchy because she has to take it easy. I'll be glad when the baby gets here."

"You're funny, DeMario. You haven't seen anything yet. The hard part is yet to come."

"I guess you're right. If I had to do it all over again, I'd be a lot more careful."

"I'm sure you would, but you can't turn back the hands of time. You and Patrice became grown in sixty seconds, without even thinking about the consequences or how it was going to affect your lives. I wasn't about to go out like that. I don't care how much I love Dré."

"Damn, girl, you sound like my momma. I know

we screwed up, but it helps that I love her and she knows I'm going to take care of my kid."

"I wouldn't expect any different from you," she replied as she opened her car door and slid into the driver's seat. "Listen, I have to get to work."

DeMario backed away from her car and said, "I'm headed to work myself. Call me later. And don't worry about these fools around here."

"I'll try," she replied as she waved good-bye.

DeMario made his way over to his car and then drove off to his job at an automotive plant, where he worked a five-hour shift with Patrice's father, five evenings a week.

Patrice closed her English book and walked into the family room, where she found her mother watching Oprah, a ritual of hers every afternoon.

"Momma, I finished my English homework."

She held out her hand and said, "Hand it to me so I can check it. While I'm doing that, start on your physical science."

"May I eat first?"

Felicia looked at the clock and said, "Yes, go ahead and eat your dinner."

Just as Patrice turned to walk away, the telephone rang. She hurried into the kitchen and answered it on the second ring. "Hello?"

"Hey, babe, what you doing?"

"I was doing homework, but I'm getting ready to eat dinner. Are you on your way to work?"

"I'm already here. I'm just sitting in the car eating a burger and listening to music before I clock in."

Patrice opened the cabinet drawer and pulled out some utensils. She removed the top on the pot and allowed the steam to rise off the turnip greens.

"How was your first day back at Langley?"

"It was okay. How's my baby? Has he done much kicking today?"

Patrice looked down at her stomach and smiled. "She's doing fine."

"It's a boy, Patrice. Stop saying *she*," he joked.

She giggled. "I thought that would get your undivided attention."

The couple talked lovingly to each other for several minutes before DeMario had to end their conversation.

"Well, I'd better get inside before Alvin comes out here looking for me with that mean look on his face," he said as he climbed out of the car.

"Daddy's not mean."

DeMario laughed as he walked toward the security gate. "You're not the one he had against the wall by the throat when he found out you were pregnant."

Patrice stirred up the red beans and said, "He was in shock, DeMario."

"Yes, and I violated Daddy's little girl."

There was silence between the two for a few seconds.

"You do know that Daddy would never hurt you, right?"

"You're trippin', Patrice. Your old man tolerates me because of you, and you know it. All I am to him is a wetback from the jungle."

Patrice's heart was wounded upon hearing DeMario's comment. "I know Daddy has his issues, but he'll just have to get over it. I love you, and that's all that matters. I'll talk to him."

"No, this is something we're going to have to work out man to man. I'll call you on my break. Love you."

"I love you too."

Patrice hung up the telephone and stared at the food her mother had prepared. All of a sudden she wasn't hungry, so she put her plate back into the cabinet and poured herself a glass of orange juice instead.

Felicia walked into the kitchen wiping tears out of her eyes.

"Oprah was off the hook today. I love me some Oprah."

When she didn't get a response out of Patrice, she did a double take and noticed she wasn't eating. "I thought you were going to eat dinner."

"I lost my appetite."

Concerned, she tilted Patrice's chin and looked into her eyes. "What's wrong? Are you feeling okay?"

"I'm fine."

"Child, I'm not stupid. I know when something's wrong," she replied as she pulled a plate out of the cabinet and started placing food on it.

"Talk to me, Patrice," Felicia demanded. "You know you have to eat to get your vitamins."

"I'm doing everything the doctor told me," she insisted.

Felicia turned and put her hand on her hip. "Then why aren't you eating?"

Figuring out that her mother was not going to leave her alone until she revealed what was bothering her, she surrendered. "DeMario feels like Daddy hates him."

Felicia set the plate of food in front of Patrice and said, "Here, eat this."

Patrice pushed the food around on the plate in silence. Felicia put a few items on her plate then sat down next to her daughter and began to explain her husband's frustrations to her daughter.

"Your father does not hate DeMario, but he is hurt that you two have altered your lives with this baby. You have to understand that your father's heart is not going to heal overnight. You have to give him time, and so does DeMario, because you did the one thing we begged you not to, and look at the result."

Tears fell out of Patrice's eyes. "I'm sorry, Momma."

Felicia dabbed Patrice's eyes with a napkin. "Baby, I know you're sorry. And don't misunderstand me; I love you, and I already love that baby. But you and DeMario have to realize that it's not easy for us as parents to act like this is not a big deal. Just give your father time. I'm sure he'll come around eventually."

"I hope you're right."

Felicia leaned over and kissed Patrice on the forehead. "I know I'm right. You're my angel and you'll always be my angel. Now, eat. You have a baby to feed."

Patrice managed to smile. Her mother had always been able to make her feel better, no matter what problems she was having.

Denim had worked with two patients before her shift was over for the evening. It was a great day, and she loved her new coworkers and boss. It was now eight o'clock, time for her to head home.

After telling everyone good night, she walked out into the lobby and greeted the security guard as he sat at his post. Denim's cell phone rang, and she pulled it out of her purse so she could answer it.

"Hello?"

"I heard something about you today. It is true?" Dré asked.

"Is what true?" She sat down on a lobby sofa.

"Don't play dumb. You know exactly what I'm talking about."

Unfortunately, so much had happened since she'd last seen Dré, she wasn't sure exactly what incident he was referring to. He could've been talking about her involvement in the gas station robbery, or he could've heard about Boomerang, or the incident in the restroom with Patience.

"Where are you?" Denim asked.

"Look outside," he replied. "I'm near the entrance of the parking lot."

Denim walked over to the glass doors and noticed Dré standing in the shadows. "Wave to me so I'll know it's really you."

Immediately, she saw his arm go up.

"I'm on my way out. Meet me at my car," she stated before walking out into the dark parking lot.

Denim put her cell back into her purse and met Dré at her car. She unlocked the door and allowed him to get in on the passenger's side. As soon as he closed the door, Denim could sense his anger.

"Can I get a hug or a kiss or something?" she asked.

Dré shook his head and said, "We need to clear up some things first."

"What things?"

"I heard that Li'l Carl's crew is claiming you."

"It's all a misunderstanding. You know I would never join a gang!"

"Why would they claim you if there wasn't a reason to?"

She laid her head against the steering wheel and

whispered, "So many crazy things have been happening to me lately, and I don't know why. You know I would never be involved with the crew."

Dré could see Denim's sadness. He should've known she wasn't in a gang, but to be sure, he had to see her reaction when he asked her.

"I'm sorry to upset you, but I had to ask. Can you forgive me?"

"Yes," she whispered softly.

"Now, talk to me. What's been going on since I last saw you?"

She leaned back and wiped a stray tear off her cheek. "I don't even know where to start."

"The beginning is always the best place."

Denim wrapped her arms around his neck and nuzzled it. "All I did was save a man's life, and now everyone's going around talking about I'm in that gang."

"You did? How?" he asked.

Denim laid her head against her headrest and began to tell Dré about the convenience store robbery, the students at school, and the incident in the restroom.

When she finished, he let out a breath, thinking about how close she came to being injured or killed. He ran his hands through her soft curls and said, "I'm glad you're safe. I had to see you and make sure you were okay."

"Thank you. I'm glad you're okay too."

He tilted her chin and brushed his lips against hers.

Their kisses were becoming quite heated—so heated that the security guard tapped on the window with his flashlight, startling the young couple. Embarrassed, Denim lowered the window.

"Are you okay, miss?" he asked.

"Yes, sir, I'm fine. I was just talking to my friend."

"Well, it looked like there was a lot more going on in there besides talking."

Denim blushed.

"I don't have to tell you two that this parking lot is not Inspiration Point, do I?

"No, sir," Dré answered with a sly grin on his face.

"Good, so you two lovebirds need to take it elsewhere," the security guard announced.

Denim turned the ignition and said, "I understand. Have a good evening."

"You too. And drive carefully," the officer replied before watching Denim drive out of the parking lot.

Once on the main highway, Denim glanced over at Dré and asked, "Where do you want to go?"

"I know where I would like to go," he replied mischievously.

"Where?" she asked with a smile.

"Somewhere very private," he answered with a serious expression on his face.

"Don't tempt me, Prime Time."

He reached over and caressed her thigh. "That's exactly what I'm trying to do."

Denim's body immediately heated up. "If you keep that up, you're going to make me have an accident."

He chuckled as he removed his hand and asked, "What time do you have to be home?"

"Why?"

"Because I can't go another day without you," he revealed.

She felt the same way. All she could think about was lying in his arms.

"Where do you want to go?" she asked.

"The usual spot, if that's okay with you."

She sped up and hurriedly drove out of town, toward the lake.

Once at the lake, Denim parked her car and the

couple exited the vehicle. She popped open the trunk and pulled out a flashlight and blanket. They made their way down through a row of trees to an embankment, until they were at the lake's edge.

Dré spread the blanket on the ground and knelt down. Denim kicked off her shoes and joined him on the blanket.

"Why am I nervous?" Dré asked.

She cupped his face and said, "Because we love each other and it's been a while. It's okay. I'm a little nervous too, but I never wanted anything or anybody like I want you."

Dré pulled Denim into his arms and kissed her hard on the lips.

"I love you Prime Time."

"I love you too, Cocoa Princess."

She kissed his neck and said, "Show me how much you love me."

Dré laid Denim back on the blanket, and for the next hour, he showed her exactly how much he loved her.

When the young couple was preparing to leave, Dré took Denim's hand into his and said, "Listen, baby. Before you leave, I've decided to tell you the reason my family is in hiding. But you can't tell a soul."

Denim could see he was struggling with his words. "I promise that anything you tell me, I'll keep it right here," she replied softly as she pointed to her heart.

Dré paced nervously back and forth in front of her before he began to reveal everything.

"You see, my dad witnessed something that he shouldn't have. Something that could get him killed. When he got jammed up on his little illegal gambling and money laundering charges, he was looking at some serious time. That's when he decided to turn state's evidence."

"What did he witness?"

"I don't know and I don't want to know. But what I do know is that whatever it is, it's big. He said whoever's involved could make us disappear with the snap of a finger. That's why he made a deal with the Feds in exchange for a new identity and a new life."

"And that's why you had to leave town so fast."

"Exactly!"

Denim couldn't believe her ears at first, but now it was all becoming clear to her. Dré had no choice of who his father was, or any choice in leaving town. Now he was risking his life just to see her, and it made her feel queasy as he continued to reveal more and more of his life on the run.

"There's a main person that my father is testifying against, and the Feds have arrested a couple of people, but there's one more person they want to get. So, until the trial comes up and everyone's in custody, we have to stay hidden."

"That's so scary. I'm so sorry I gave you a hard time."

He kissed her gently on the lips and said, "It's cool, but I have to be extra careful. The Feds would be pissed if they knew I was coming back into town, talking to you and DeMario. They wanted to put a monitoring device on me to keep up with me, but I wasn't going for that.

"Now can't you see why I don't want you involved in any way? I couldn't live with myself if something happened to you."

"That's so scary," she said as she caressed his arm. "I don't want you to put yourself at risk anymore by coming to see me. I understand now."

He smiled and then reached over and played with a strand of her hair. "I knew you would, but don't worry about me I've gotten good at moving around in the shadows."

"What about school and basketball?"

"I had to give up basketball because my picture might end up in the newspaper and that would lead the bad people right to us, but I am in school."

"I know how much you love playing basketball. It has to be hard to give it up."

"That's okay. I'll get another chance," he said as he pulled her up into his arms. "Let's go. It's getting late."

Denim drove back into town in silence. Her mind was trying to register all the information Dré had revealed, and it had her in a daze.

Dré reached over and played with a strand of her hair. He whispered, "I'm coming back to you, baby, just as soon as I can. Being with you tonight was unbelievable—better than I remembered."

She blushed. "Then I can't wait until we can hook up again. I have goose bumps on my arms."

"I'm addicted to you, Denim Mitchell."

"I'm addicted to you too."

He closed his eyes and smiled with satisfaction. He had his woman back, but he was still missing something that was very important to him—basketball.

* * *

When Denim got home, she pulled her diary out of her book bag and made an entry. As she wrote, she decided to leave out the part about Dré's situation, just in case her diary fell into the wrong hands.

Dear Diary,

Dré mysteriously showed up at my job tonight. Lawd, that man is fine. Anyway, he came to see me because he heard the rumors at school about my association with the crew. After I told him what happened at the gas station, he realized the truth behind the rumors. We took our conversation out to the lake and well, what can I say? We were all over each other, to say the least. Dré knows EXACTLY what to do to me and how to do it. Just the thought of him right now has my body trembling. I can't wait to see him again.

Later,
D

Chapter Nine

The pain Patrice felt in her head when she woke up was unbelievable. As she tried to stand up, the room started to spin. Then, just before she was able to call out to her mother for help, she collapsed unconscious on the floor. Thirty minutes would go by before her mother would find her, leaving Patrice in the fight for not only her life, but that of her unborn baby.

Denim was making her way through the hallway to her second period class when DeMario ran up to her frantically and grabbed her arm. As he pulled her down the hallway, he yelled, "Denim! It's Patrice! She's sick! I have to get to her. I need you! Help me!"

Denim had no idea what was going on. When

they got to the exit, she was able to stop DeMario temporarily. "Slow down, DeMario, you're not making any sense. What's wrong with Patrice?"

He took a breath and said, "Her mom called and said she found Patrice unconscious on the floor of her bedroom. They're on their way to the hospital. Come with me!"

Denim's heart went out DeMario. She wanted to cry, but she knew she had to stay strong for him. "Come on, we'll take my car."

DeMario and Denim ran out of the school and across the parking lot to her car. They jumped in and sped off to the hospital as quickly as possible.

At the hospital, Denim and DeMario were met by Patrice's parents. They could tell by the look on their faces that it wasn't good.

DeMario asked, "Where's Patrice? Is the baby okay?"

"The doctors are with her now," Felicia revealed. "She's in bad shape, DeMario. She has toxemia."

"She's going to be okay, right? What about the baby?" he asked.

DeMario was frantic and he needed answers. He couldn't lose Patrice and the baby. He just couldn't.

Patrice's father put his hand on DeMario's shoulder and said, "Calm down, son. You're not going to do Patrice any good being upset like this."

"No! I want to see Patrice!"

Felicia hugged DeMario and said, "Sit down, DeMario. The doctors are doing everything they can to save them. Right now all we can do is pray, because it's in God's hands."

DeMario sat down and covered his face with his hands. He was obviously crying, and Denim did what she could to comfort him. She sat down beside him and put her arm around his shoulders.

"Don't worry, DeMario. Patrice and the baby will be okay," she whispered.

Denim looked over at Patrice's parents and asked, "Is there anything I can do for you guys?"

Felicia forced a smile and said softly, "You're already doing it, Denim. Thanks for coming. Patrice would be happy to know you're here."

At that moment, the doctor exited the emergency room and walked over to the family. Denim had a feeling the news wasn't going to be good. They all stood and waited for the news of Patrice's condition.

"Mr. and Mrs. Fontenot, Patrice is in critical condition. The toxemia has set up in her body, and we have to deliver the baby right away if she's going to have any chance of survival."

"After you deliver the baby, is she going to be okay?" Alvin asked.

"That's what we're hoping for, but we have to deliver the baby first, and then we'll know more about where we stand."

DeMario asked, "Can I see her? Please, I need to see her."

The doctor smiled and said, "You can see her once she comes out of recovery. Right now, time is of the essence, and we have to have your permission to act right away. We're doing everything we can to save both of them. I'll come back down once we deliver the baby."

"Of course, doctor. Do whatever you have to, to save my daughter and the baby," Alvin replied as they walked over to the nurse's station to sign the required paperwork.

Denim was speechless and hurt, so she could only imagine what DeMario and the Fontenots were feeling. The last thing she wanted was to have something happen to Patrice and her baby before she had a change to apologize to her.

"DeMario, I don't know what to say. Can I get you anything?"

"No, I'm cool."

"I need to call Dré. He would want to be here. How do you contact him?"

DeMario gave her his cell phone and told her the code name he had him programmed under.

Denim stepped away from the family and dialed the number. Dré answered almost immediately. He was surprised that it was Denim on the telephone instead of DeMario, but the minute he heard her voice, he knew that something was wrong.

Denim explained the circumstances to him, and then after hanging up, she returned to DeMario's side and said, "Dré's on his way."

"I can't lose her, Denim."

"And you won't," she replied as she hugged his neck.

Fifteen minutes later, doctors delivered a five-pound baby boy by caesarean section. Relief swept over everyone; however, Patrice was still in critical condition, and now in a coma.

DeMario couldn't do anything but cry when he laid eyes on his son for the first time. As he stared at him through the glass, he said, "He looks like Patrice."

"He looks like both of you," Denim replied.

Denim smiled. "He's so cute. What name did you guys pick out for him?"

"We were leaning toward Alejandro."

"Alejandro. I like that. What if it had been a girl?"

"We were going to name her Janisa."

Denim looked at her watch and said, "I see. So, are you going to name him Alejandro?"

"I'm going to wait until Patrice wakes up so we can do it together. She had a few other names she was tossing around too. We never said definitely what we were going to name him."

"I think that's a great idea," Denim replied as she linked her arm with his. "So, are you going to go in there and hold your son?"

"I want to, but I want Patrice to hold him first."

"That's cool, DeMario, but you need to start bonding with him."

At that time, Dré rounded the corner and joined the pair. After hugging DeMario, he hugged and kissed Denim, putting a huge smile on her face.

"How's Patrice?" he asked.

DeMario leaned against the wall and said, "She's in a coma and the doctors don't know when she's going to wake up."

"You know Patrice is too mean to stay asleep

long, bro. Besides, I'm sure she's just as anxious as I am to see you change diapers."

DeMario and Denim laughed at Dré's comment.

"You're right about that one," DeMario replied.

Dré looked through the window at the newborns. "Which one is yours?"

"He's in the first row, second one from the left."

"Wow! A boy! Congratulations, man! He's huge!"

"Thanks, bro. Don't you think he looks like Patrice?"

"Just a little bit. Have you held him yet?"

"Not yet."

"Well, get in there. What are you waiting on?" Dré asked.

"He wanted to wait until Patrice wakes up," Denim announced.

"Patrice is going to be mad if she wakes up and finds out you haven't held your son yet, and you know it," Dré added. "Get your ass in there and let your son know who his daddy is."

DeMario nodded and then tapped on the glass to get the nurse's attention. Denim and Dré watched through the window as DeMario was directed into a second room, where he slid into a surgical gown and held his son for the first time.

*   *   *

Denim left the hospital only so she could get in her hours at work. She hated leaving the Fontenots, DeMario, and especially Dré, but this was a new job and she didn't want to jeopardize it. Before going into the building, she made a journal entry in her diary.

Dear Diary,

Today was a good day and a bad day. Patrice got sick from the toxemia. She had to have an emergency C-section to deliver her beautiful son, but unfortunately, Patrice is now in a coma. DeMario is devastated, but I told him he had to be strong for Patrice and his son. I'm praying that everything works out and that Patrice wakes up soon so I can apologize to her.

Later,
D

Denim closed her diary and entered the building so she could hurry through her shift.

After working with her three patients, Denim hurried back to the hospital to be with her friends.

When she arrived, she found out that Patrice's condition hadn't improved and she was still in a coma.

She sat down between Dré and DeMario and asked, "How are you holding up? Have you eaten?"

"I had to force him down to the cafeteria a couple of hours ago," Dré revealed.

"Did he eat?" she asked.

"Stop talking about me like I'm not sitting here," he complained.

"We're just worried about you," Denim explained. "You have to eat."

"I'm fine," he replied as he stood and walked over to the window.

"He's not fine, Denim," Dré whispered to her. "He's barely hanging on."

"Has he seen Patrice yet?" she asked.

"Yeah, he saw her, but only for a few minutes. He said she's hooked up to a lot of medical equipment. Seeing her like that got to him, and he basically fell apart when he came out of her room."

Felicia Fontenot exited Patrice's room and walked over to the teens. "Why don't you kids go home and get some rest. If anything changes in Patrice's condition, we'll give you a call."

Denim looked at her watch and noticed that it

was getting close to ten o'clock, and she knew she had to go to school the next day. She stood and said, "Mrs. Felicia, I'll keep praying for Patrice. Call me if you need anything."

Felicia kissed Denim's forehead and smiled. "I will. Go home and get some rest and tell your parents I said hello."

"I will, and my mom said she'll be here in the morning to see you."

"I'd like that," Felicia replied.

Denim walked over to the window and stood next to DeMario. "I'm getting ready to go home, but I'll be back after school tomorrow. You call me if you need anything—and I mean *anything*."

He turned and hugged her tightly. "Thanks for being here."

"You know I wouldn't have it any other way. Try to get some rest, and kiss the baby for me."

"Will do," DeMario answered.

Dré walked over to the pair and said, "I'll walk you out."

Dré patted DeMario on the shoulder and said, "I'll be back in a second."

DeMario nodded but continued to stare out the window.

* * *

Downstairs, Dré walked Denim to her car. The night air was chilly, and Denim had forgotten her jacket. As she shivered, Dré pulled her closer, to warm her body.

"Is DeMario going to be okay?" she asked as she snuggled up to him.

"Yeah, he's just scared, but I'm sure Patrice will pull through."

"It's my fault," Denim whispered. "I should've been there for her. Maybe if I had, she wouldn't be lying upstairs in a coma."

Dré held her close as they stood by her car. "Patrice is not in a coma because of you. Do you have any idea how silly that sounds?"

Denim looked up into Dré's eyes. "I still could've been a better friend to her. If I had, maybe I could've kept her from getting sick."

"Be her friend now. It's not too late. She's going to need you if she's going to have any chance of pulling through."

"I guess you're right. I'd better get going. Make sure you call me if anything changes."

He tightened his arms around her and kissed her softly on the lips. "No doubt, Cocoa Princess. Drive safely."

"I will," she answered as she slid in behind the wheel of her car and turned on the heat.

After he watched her drive off, Dré made his way back over to the hospital, but before he was able to step up on the sidewalk, a car came to a screeching halt, blocking his path. Dré froze when he stared down the barrel of a nine millimeter handgun.

"Get in the car!" the man yelled.

Chapter Ten

Dana Patterson sat in the family room with her heart pounding in her chest. She couldn't believe her ears. Her husband had agreed to let the Feds use Dré as bait to catch their last suspect.

"What the hell were you thinking, Garrett? Dré is our son! Don't you love him at all?"

"Of course I love my son! I'm doing this so we can get our lives back."

"Then why didn't you use yourself as bait? You're the one they want, not Dré! I hate you!" she yelled.

Agent Miller interrupted, saying, "Mrs. Patterson, Dré is our best hope in flushing out the suspect. If we had used Garrett, they would've smelled a setup a mile away."

"So what? You have my son out there with a target on his chest!" Dana yelled. "Does he know?"

"No, he doesn't know, but we have agents—"

Dana put her hand up to stop the agent from speaking. "Now, you listen to me. My son went to the hospital to visit a friend who might die, and you two sit here and tell me that if things go bad, I could lose my own child?"

"It's not like that, Dana. Dré is being protected. It's not like he hasn't been sneaking back into town anyway. He's been putting himself in danger all along without our knowledge."

"Garrett, you and Agent Miller can go to hell!"

"They're not going to let anything happen to him."

Dana stood and put her finger in her husband's face. "If anything happens to my son, you can forget about us, because I'm going to take him as far away from you as I can!"

Garrett lowered his head in shame as Dana stormed out of the room and into her bedroom, slamming the door behind her. Agent Miller leaned closer to Garrett.

"Mr. Patterson, Dré will be fine. I promise. Our agents have done this type of operation many times, and they have a very high success rate."

Garrett balled up his fists and said, "They'd better be experts, or there will be hell to pay."

"You have to trust us."

"No! All I have to do is live and die!" Garrett yelled. "You just make sure you return my son to me in one piece, and I want the thugs who have a personal interest in me locked up for life!"

"That's what we're trying to do, Mr. Patterson."

Now it was Garrett's turn to point fingers. "If this thing is not finished in the next twenty-four hours and my son back home safe, the whole deal is off."

Agent Miller nodded. "We're doing everything we can."

"Man, you don't have a clue!" Garrett yelled. "I could lose my wife and son over this mess."

"May I remind you that *you* put yourself in this position, not us."

Garrett looked in the direction of his bedroom and said, "Yeah, whatever, man."

"Don't you think you need to go check on Mrs. Patterson?" Agent Miller asked as he poured himself a cup of coffee.

"You let me worry about my wife. She's okay. She just needs some time to cool off."

What Garrett didn't know was that Dana was fed up and in the bedroom packing her belongings.

* * *

Dré couldn't believe he was staring down the barrel of a gun. His parents' nightmares had finally come true.

"Get in the car, kid, and don't make me tell you again."

Dré glanced over at the hospital door. He was only a few feet away, and if he made a run for it, he just might make it without getting shot.

The back door swung open on the car and a large African American man exited the vehicle.

"I said get in the damn car!"

Before Dré could react, two cars with blue lights flashing quickly pulled in, blocking the gunman's car. Several men jumped out of the car with their guns drawn and shouted orders at the men in the car.

"Drop the gun! Get on the ground!"

Dré put his hands up in the air because he wasn't trying to get shot. As he stood there, he watched in amazement, as federal agents swarmed the gunman's vehicle. The driver of the car was pulled from the vehicle and immediately thrown to the ground. The gunman dropped the handgun and was also thrown to the ground.

One of the agents walked over to Dré and asked, "Are you okay?"

Still somewhat in shock, Dré said, "I think so."

"Are you hurt anywhere?" he asked as he inspected Dré's body.

"No, sir, I'm fine. Who are you?"

"We work with Agent Miller. He had us tail you to keep you safe. I'm Agent Rivera."

Dré sat on the curb and asked, "Why didn't he tell me?"

"He thought it was best that you didn't know. We found out from a reliable source that these men have been tailing your friend, DeMario, hoping he would lead them to you. We weren't sure when they would make their move, so we tailed him as well. That's how things ended up here."

Dré held his head in his hands. "I can't believe this. How long have you been following me?"

"For a few weeks now," the agent revealed.

At that moment, Dré realized that the agents probably witnessed his romantic interlude with Denim at the lake.

"Did my parents know you were following me?" Dré asked.

"Only your father knew. We didn't want to compromise the operation by telling your mother."

"So does this mean we're safe now?" Dré asked.

"Agent Miller will brief you on the specifics. For now, we need to get you back home," the agent said as he took Dré by the arm.

"I can't leave. DeMario's expecting me to come back."

"You can call him from the car," Agent Rivera replied.

Dré looked over at the hospital doors. "That's not good enough. Can I at least go upstairs and tell him I have to leave?"

Agent Rivera waved another officer over and said, "Yes, but make it quick. Agent Windrow, accompany this young man upstairs to see his friend. Give him no more than five minutes, and then take him to the field office."

"Yes, sir," he answered before escorting Dré upstairs.

Minutes later, Dré sat in the waiting room with DeMario and Patrice's parents. While Agent Windrow watched, Dré quickly said his good-byes and told them as much as he could in five minutes.

When he was finished, DeMario gave him a brotherly hug and said, "I'm glad it's over for you and your family."

"Me too," Dré replied as he released DeMario and shook Mr. Fontenot's hand.

Felicia hugged Dré and said, "Take care of yourself."

"Yes, ma'am."

Agent Windrow motioned for Dré to join him, so he stood and hugged DeMario once more before stepping onto the elevator with the agent.

Tears fell from Denim's eyes as she held her cell phone up to her ear, listening as he explained what happened in the hospital parking lot after she left. She couldn't believe how close Dré had come to being kidnapped.

"It's really over, Cocoa Princess."

"Are you sure?" she asked.

"It's the truth. It's finally over. I love you, Denim, and we don't have to sneak around anymore to be together."

She closed her eyes and softly whispered, "I love the sound of that."

"Me too, sweetheart."

Dré looked at Agent Windrow, who pointed at his watch.

"I have to go before this agent has a stroke. I'll be in touch with you as soon as I can."

"I can't wait. I love you."

Denim closed her cell phone and fell back on her bed with a huge smile on her face. She immediately pulled out her diary to record the latest events.

Dear Diary,

This has been and up and down day emotionally for me. Patrice is still in a coma, and I haven't been there for her as a friend in a long time. Now she needs me more than ever, and I just don't know what to do.

On another note, Dré called with some great news. It seems like he's coming home and life can get back to normal. I can't put it in writing, but he and his family have been through hell.

I'm so happy for Dré, but tonight my prayers will be for Patrice, that she wakes up soon.

Later,
D

Just as Denim put her diary back in the nightstand, a picture of her, DeMario, Patrice and Dré fell out from the pages. She picked up the photograph they had taken a year ago in the mall. Denim particularly noted the joy on Patrice's face as she held on to DeMario.

"This is crazy," Denim mumbled to herself as she slid the picture back inside the pages of her diary. Her mind was now racing. There was no way she would be able to sleep, because her mind was now consumed with thoughts of Patrice and the guilt she carried in her heart.

Hours passed, and it was now nearing midnight. She needed some peace in order to regain her sanity, so she reached over and picked up her cell phone and dialed DeMario's number.

"Hello?" he answered in a hoarse voice.

"I didn't mean to wake you. How's Patrice?"

He wiped his eyes and sat up. "She's the same. Her blood pressure is still up and she's still in a coma. I tried talking to her, but it's not doing any good."

Denim paced the floor nervously. "How's the baby?"

"He's perfect," he whispered proudly. "Why aren't you asleep?"

"I can't sleep. I feel like I need to be there with you and Patrice."

He looked at his watch and said, "Well, it's late

and you've been here all day. There's no reason for you to come back out tonight."

"I'm worried about Patrice."

"I'm worried about Patrice, too, but like Mrs. Felicia said, it's in God's hands."

Denim knew she had to have faith and believe that God would take care of Patrice, but human nature still caused her to worry.

"I'm still praying for her. Did Dré tell you what happened tonight?"

"Yeah, he's one lucky brotha."

"I'm just glad his drama seems to be over so he can come back to school."

"And back to you, huh?" DeMario teased.

"You got that right. I've missed him so much."

They laughed together.

"Seriously, Denim, I'm good, and I promise you if anything changes, I'll give you a call. Now go to bed. Okay?"

"You don't have to twist my arm. I'll stop by in the morning before I go to school and bring you guys some breakfast."

"Now, that sounds great. I'm sure Patrice would love to hear your voice too."

"I'd like that."

"Good. Now, good night."

Chapter Eleven

Felicia Fontenot had been playing Patrice's favorite songs for days now; however, nothing seemed to be working to bring her out of the coma.

Denim had come by each day to visit and to bring DeMario his homework assignments. Unfortunately, she still hadn't found the strength to spend any private time with Patrice. Guilt still consumed her, and she thought her visit would do more harm to Patrice than good.

"Denim, I really appreciate you helping me keep up with my homework."

She handed him a Quiznos sandwich and a napkin and smiled. "It's no problem. Besides, I can't have you flunking out of school. You need to get that diploma so you can go to college."

DeMario looked down at the sandwich and

rubbed his stomach in anticipation. "College seems so far away, but I know it's just around the corner. Thanks again for the sandwich. You know Quiznos is my favorite."

"I remembered. I also knew you weren't going to leave the hospital to get one for yourself."

The pair sat there and enjoyed their sandwiches in silence while they watched music videos on the TV. Denim finished half of her sandwich and then wrapped the rest of it up and put it back in the bag.

"I brought a couple of sandwiches for Mr. Alvin and Mrs. Felicia too. I hope they like them, because I had no idea what to order for them."

DeMario looked down in the bag and asked, "What did you get?"

"I got Mr. Alvin a prime rib sandwich, and Mrs. Felicia's sandwich has chicken on it."

"They'll like it. None of us have really been eating since we got here."

"I figured that," Denim responded. "What about your job, DeMario? Have you talked to your boss?"

"I did, and Patrice's dad worked things out so I could stay here with Patrice without being penalized."

Denim looked around and asked, "Where are they, anyway?"

"Mrs. Felicia's in the room with Patrice. She made Mr. Alvin go home so he could take a shower and a nap. They're going to take turns staying with Patrice."

"What about you?" Denim asked before changing the channel on the TV.

"I'm not leaving her," he quickly answered.

Denim set the remote control down on the table and sighed. "You can't stay here twenty-four-seven. You have to go home and shower at some point."

"I'm not leaving her," he repeated as he pulled a pickle off his sandwich and popped it into his mouth.

Denim smiled and pinched her nose with her fingers. "You need a shower, DeMario. You're getting pretty tart."

They laughed together.

"Seriously, though, I promise, if you go home, shower, and get some rest, I'll stay here with Patrice until you get back."

He took another bite of his sandwich without responding. Denim watched his facial expressions and wondered what he was thinking.

"Are you going to take me up on my offer or not?"

"I'm afraid to leave her. I want to be here when she wakes up."

"You will be, but do you want to be incoherent when she does wake up? You need some real rest."

"I can't believe she's still in a coma. We've tried everything to get her to wake up. We've talked to her, played her favorite songs, and even placed the baby in the bed with her, but nothing's working. I'm starting to think she'll never wake up."

"Don't start thinking like that. Give her a little more time. I'm sure she'll be awake and fussing at you in no time," Denim said to try to cheer him up.

"I hope you're right. I'd give anything to hear her yell at me right now."

Denim nodded in agreement.

"So, how's things with Dré?" DeMario asked to change the subject.

"I haven't seen him, but I talked to him. He said his family has been going through some type of debriefing before they move back to town."

"I know you can't wait, can you?"

She rubbed her arms and said, "Just the thought of it gives me goose bumps.

Now, will you please go home and take a shower?"

"Okay, stop nagging. I'll go, but I'll be right back," he replied as he stood.

She handed him the keys to her car and picked up a magazine. "Take your time, and make sure you lather up real good."

Tears filled his eyes. "Thanks for hanging around."

"You're welcome, now go," she replied as she waved him away.

For the past few days, Dré and his family had been packing up their belongings in preparation to move back to town. The movers had already transported their large items to their new home. All that was left were small items and their clothes.

After several days of debriefing by the Feds, Dré finally felt like his life was on the road to recovery. The first order of business was to see Denim. The second would be to call his coach to see about getting back on the basketball team. He felt bad that he hadn't had the opportunity to get back to the hospital to see Patrice, but he'd been in constant contact with DeMario and sent his blessings.

Dré walked into the living room with two suitcases in his hands. He set them down near the front door and went into the kitchen to search for his mother. He found her carefully wrapping up her crystal glasses and other fragile items.

"Momma, I've packed all my clothes. Is it okay if I go to the house and start unpacking?"

Dana smiled at her son. "Who do you think you're fooling? I know you're in a hurry to get back to town to see Denim."

Dré blushed. His mother had seen right through him. "Can you blame me?"

Dana walked over to Dré and cupped his face. "No, I can't blame you."

Dré hugged his mother.

"Take it slow, son," she replied as she stepped out of his embrace. "I don't want you and Denim ending up like Patrice and DeMario. Do you hear me?"

Dré went over to the refrigerator and pulled out a can of Coke. "Come on, Momma. You know I'm a virgin."

Dana giggled. "Please, Dré. I'm your mother, which means there isn't much that you can get past me."

"What do you think you know?" Dré asked with a smirk on his face.

"Oh, I know everything, sweetheart. In fact, I've had a nanny cam in the house for a couple of years now, so guess how surprised I was at the footage it taped of you and Denim."

Dré nearly dropped the Coke he was holding in his hand.

"You had what put in the house?" he asked nervously.

Dana could see the blood drain from his face. "A nanny cam," she replied. "You know, a hidden camera."

"Stop playing. Daddy wouldn't let you put a camera in the house," he replied as he took a sip of Coke.

She winked at him and whispered, "He never knew about it either."

Dré started coughing uncontrollably. He nearly choked on his soda.

"Are you okay, Dré?" Dana asked as she gave him a pat on the back.

"I'm cool. I just can't believe you would put a spy cam in your own home," he pointed out as he took another sip of Coke to moisten his dry throat.

Dana laughed and then said, "I'm just joking about the camera, but I'm serious when I say don't make me a grandmother."

This time, Dana wasn't smiling, which meant she was actually being serious about her request.

"I hear you, Momma."

"Don't just hear me, son. I know I've said it a hundred times before, but I want to make sure you understand how serious I am about this."

"Yes, ma'am."

"Good, because you and I have always been able to be up front with each other, and I don't ever want that to change. Okay?"

"Okay. Can I go now?"

"Yes, you can go. Drive carefully, and call me when you get to the house."

Before leaving the room, Dré turned to his mother and reluctantly asked, "Have you talked to Daddy?"

Dana stopped packing the crystal and looked into her son's eyes. "Yes, I've talked to him."

"Are you guys really breaking up?"

"It's complicated, Dré. I love your father, but this ordeal was too much for me. I need some time to think, and I can't do that with your father around."

"I don't want to see you guys break up, but I want you to be happy, so whatever you decide, I'm cool."

"Thank you. And whatever happens, remember Garrett is and will always be your father."

Dré threw the empty Coke can into the trash. "I will. I love you, Momma."

Dana continued to pack her crystal. "I love you too."

Garrett pulled the picture of his family out of his wallet and stared at it as he sat in the field office. His heart thumped in his chest as he looked at Dana's beautiful face. She looked so happy in the picture; now, thanks to him, he was on the verge of losing the only woman he'd ever loved.

"Dana," he whispered. "I'm so sorry."

Agent Miller entered the room and noticed the picture. "Mr. Patterson, we have a new place all set up for you. Are you ready to go?"

"I'm as ready as I'm going to be," he replied as he slid the picture back inside his wallet.

"I'm sure the stress of this case has taken a toll on you and your family, but I'm sure you'll be back with them in no time."

"I wish I was as sure as you are, Agent Miller," he answered as he put his wallet in his back pocket. "Show me this place you have for me, so I can get on with my life."

"Mr. Patterson, please don't give up on your family. You're doing a good thing for the community, and especially yourself. You have to remember that an undercover federal agent was killed. Agent

Gilbert was a young man, and he had a family just like yours. Your testimony is necessary against the people responsible."

"I understand all that, Agent Miller."

"Then understand this. The man who murdered that agent will kill again if you don't put him away. I know you didn't expect to walk in on the murder, but you did, and there's no turning back now."

Garrett looked at Agent Miller in silence. He'd known the triggerman, C-Note, all his life, and had he not stopped by C-Note's place to handle his gambling business, he would be behind bars and the Feds would be looking at an unsolved murder right now.

"That doesn't make me feel any better." Garrett put his hands over his face and then asked, "Why didn't that agent have any backup?"

"He'd been successful working the way he did. Superiors pleaded with him to allow some type of support, but he was against it."

"Look where that got him," Garrett replied. "How can I show my face in town again? I'm labeled as a snitch now."

"We offered to relocate you and your family anywhere you wanted to go."

"My family has other plans."

Agent Miller patted Garrett on the shoulder and said, "It'll work out. You'll see."

Denim met Dré at his new house and he gave her the full tour. This house was similar to the house they were living in now, and he couldn't wait to settle in.

"So, what do you think?" he asked.

She sat on the bed and crossed her legs. Dré's eyes immediately went down to her shapely body. She was wearing a short denim skirt and white button-down blouse.

"I like it. Your room is larger than your old one."

"You noticed. I'm planning on putting a loveseat in here, so when I want to chill, I don't have to be on the bed."

Denim looked around the room and said, "I like that idea."

"Are you going to help me break it in?" He put one arm around her shoulders while his other hand caressed her cheek.

"What? The loveseat, or your room?

He gently kissed her neck and whispered, "Both."

She blushed and stood. "Dré, the movers are in the other room."

He lay back on the bed and said, "Once I close this door, they're not going to come in here."

"You're serious, aren't you?"

He pulled her into his arms. "Can you blame me? We have a lot of catching up to do."

"There's nothing more that I want right now but to feel your warm skin again mine, but I can't concentrate with everything that's going on with Patrice."

Dré kissed her neck once more and said, "I know you're worried about her, but so am I. What's the best way to relieve stress?"

She laid her head against his chest in silence and then said, "As bad as I want to, I just can't, Dré."

He caressed her back and then said, "I'll make a deal with you."

"What kind of deal?" she asked with tears in her eyes.

"We'll go visit Patrice together, and once she wakes up, you're all mine. Deal?"

Denim threw her arms around Dré's neck and kissed him lovingly on the lips as they fell onto his bed. "Deal! Thank you, Prime Time."

He quickly ran his hands under her skirt and touched her. Denim closed her eyes and sucked in a breath.

"Mercy," Dré whispered.

"Dré, you're not playing fair."

"I almost forgot how good you felt in my hands," he answered with a strained voice.

Denim had to admit that his hands were doing a number on her, and she came very close to giving in to him, especially when she felt the evidence of his desire for her.

"Dré, we have to stop."

"Okay, get off me before I roll you onto your back and break the deal I just made with you."

Denim giggled, but before moving, she whispered, "Dré, I promise you, when Patrice wakes up, I'm going to give you a housewarming gift that you'll never forget."

When Denim tried to get up, Dré held her in place on top of his body.

"Denim, you have no idea what you're doing to me right now."

She kissed him softly on the lips and said, "Oh, I know, and I promise you, it'll be worth the wait."

Dré pushed her off his body and said, "Get your jacket. We're going to the hospital now so I can slap Patrice awake."

Denim giggled as she followed Dré out of the house and to his car.

Chapter Twelve

Patrice's condition had gotten worse since Denim's last visit. Even though she'd delivered the baby, her blood pressure had actually elevated, causing Patrice to have a violent seizure.

"DeMario, what are the doctors saying?" Denim asked.

"I don't know. Some kind of mumbo jumbo about her blood vessels. I freaked out when I saw her."

"What are they going to do now?" Dré asked.

"They're going to give her some more medicine. They're trying to keep her from having a stroke."

"Oh, no!" Denim yelled before she started sobbing.

Dré pulled her into his arms to comfort her.

"This has been a nightmare," DeMario whispered. "I'm going to see the baby. I'll be back shortly."

"Take your time, bro," Dré replied.

Once DeMario was gone, Dré pleaded with Denim to pull herself together. In crisis situations, it was very important for the people around to stay positive.

"Babe, you can't fall apart around DeMario. It's hard enough for him as it is. We have to help him keep his spirits up."

"I'll try, but it's not going to be easy."

He tilted her chin so he could see her eyes. "Have you talked to Patrice?"

She shook her head and whispered, "No. I can't."

Dré stood and pulled Denim out of her chair. He took her by the hand and pulled her toward the hallway. "Come on."

"Where are you taking me?"

"You need to talk to Patrice."

"Wait, Dré!" she yelled as she pulled away from him.

"It's now or never, Denim. You've stalled long enough."

"I don't know what to say to her," she admitted.

He held her hand lovingly and said, "She's your friend. I'm sure the words will come to you."

She wiped her eyes with a tissue and then nodded.

He kissed her on the lips and said, "Just relax. I'm going to check on DeMario and the baby. Handle your business, sweetheart, and be yourself. Okay?"

"Okay," she replied.

Denim watched as Dré disappeared around the corner to join DeMario, and then she took a deep breath and walked into Patrice's room. She found Felicia Fontenot putting Vaseline on Patrice's lips. Her father was sitting in a chair reading a *Sports Illustrated* magazine.

"Hey, Denim," Felicia greeted her. "Come on in."

Mr. Fontenot stood and said, "You can sit here."

She waved him off and said, "No, you stay there. I'd rather stand."

Denim had a hard time looking at Patrice, who looked somewhat bloated. "How is she?"

"Better than she was earlier," Felicia answered. "Did DeMario tell you about the seizure?"

"Yes, ma'am. I'm so sorry."

"Thank you," Felicia replied with a smile, and then she noticed Denim's anxiety. She walked over to her and cupped her face. "Have you been crying?"

"Yes, ma'am."

Felicia hugged her. "I knew you still cared about Patrice. You guys have been friends for too long to let some silly rift come between you. She really has missed you."

"It's my fault, Mrs. Fontenot. I'm sorry I haven't been there for her."

"What are you talking about? It's nobody's fault. These things happen sometimes. Would you like some time alone with her?"

Backing away, Denim stuttered, "I don't want to interfere."

"You're not interfering, Denim. You're family, so you belong here. Alvin, let's go grab something from the cafeteria so we can give Denim some time with Patrice."

Alvin set his magazine on the chair and said, "We'll be right back, okay?"

"Yes, sir."

Denim waited until the Fontenots left the room before she approached the bed. She walked over to Patrice and sat down in the chair closest to her. As she sat there, she listened to the sounds of the machines she was hooked up to.

"Wow, Patrice, you really know how to get somebody's attention."

She picked up a stack of CDs and searched through them. A smile appeared on her face when she found the Rihanna and Chris Brown CDs. They were Patrice's favorites. She put the Chris Brown CD in the CD player and pushed play. As the music began to play, Denim started bopping her head to the beat.

"Patrice, do you remember this song? We danced to it in the school talent show."

Denim smiled and got up out of the chair and started performing the dance routine. "Come on, Patrice. You remember the steps, don't you?"

She continued to dance and seemed to get lost in her own world. It felt good to dance to something familiar. It had been a while since she'd danced, and today it felt so good.

"Patrice, I bet you can't do this move," she teased as she continued to dance around the room. When the song ended, Denim sat down in the chair, out of breath.

"I'm out of shape. I need to dance more often."

Denim looked over at Patrice and still saw no response. She scooted the chair closer to Patrice's bed and said, "You know, Patrice, you really need to wake up because Dré is planning on coming in here to slap you if you don't wake up. We made a deal today, and it involves a lot of sweating and heavy breathing, if you know what I mean. But that won't happen as long as you're asleep, so wake up."

Still no response.

"Okay, I see you're going to play hard. Listen, what do I have to do to get your butt out of this bed?"

Silence still engulfed the room, except for the beeping of the machines. Denim reached over and reluctantly took Patrice's hand into hers. Her skin was warm and soft, just like she remembered.

"Patrice, your son is very handsome. I know you can't wait to see him. DeMario thinks he looks like you, but I see DeMario all over him. You did good, girl. Now, wake up so you can hold that handsome little man of yours. Besides, I don't think DeMario knows a thing about changing diapers."

She caressed Patrice's arm in silence.

A nurse walked into the room and looked at Patrice's chart.

"Do you need me to leave?" Denim asked.

"No, you're fine. I just came in to change her IV bag."

Denim watched as the nurse went about her routine.

"Are you family?"

The question caught Denim off guard. "No. Well, sort of. We've been best friends since we were little."

"I see," the nurse replied. "You're a good friend to stay with her while her parents take a break."

"Thank you," Denim whispered.

The nurse changed the IV bag, checked Patrice's incision, and left the room.

Denim looked at Patrice's face and whispered, "Patrice, if you can hear me, I want to let you know that I'm sorry for everything. I'm sorry I got mad at you for something so stupid and letting you down when you needed me the most. Now, wake up so you can curse me out for being so selfish."

Denim waited for a response, any response, but it never came.

The Fontenots returned to the room an hour later and smiled when they saw Denim holding Patrice's hand.

"Anything?" Mrs. Fontenot asked.

"No, ma'am," Denim replied as she released Patrice's hand. "It's time for me to get to work, but I'll back tomorrow to spend a little more time with her."

Mr. Fontenot picked up his magazine and casually said, "Drive carefully, sweetheart. We'll see you tomorrow."

Tomorrow came and so did the next day, and so on. Patrice was still in a coma, but her vital signs had improved tremendously. The baby had been discharged from the hospital, and Alvin and De-Mario went back to work with a lot of resistance. Felicia stayed with Patrice and kept the baby by her side so he could get used to his mother. De-Mario still refused to officially name the baby until Patrice woke up, so in the meantime, everyone gave him their own nickname.

Denim visited every night after work. She kept up with the daily events in her diary and continued to talk to Patrice and play all her favorite songs.

Dré was back in school and on the basketball team, which made both of them happy, especially the coach. His parents were still estranged, and his father was in the middle of the murder trial. Dré missed his dad being around the house, but he did enjoy seeing his mother happy.

What made him happiest of all was the fact that Denim had given in to their deal one Saturday afternoon when his mom went to visit Patrice and the Fontenots. Denim kept her word on making their sensual encounter worth the wait, and she felt closer to him than she ever had.

Spending time with Patrice had melted away a lot of the anger and bitterness Denim had held inside for so long. Now, making amends with Patrice would be her ultimate satisfaction.

Nearly three months had passed since Patrice fell into the coma. Her vitals were finally normal and her neurology exams came back clear, but for some reason, she was still in a coma.

Felicia Fontenot had to take the baby to his checkup, and DeMario and Alvin had to work. Denim volunteered to skip her last class so she could sit with Patrice.

When she walked into the room, Denim held up the new Chris Brown CD. "Patrice, you're going to love me. I have your boy's latest CD. It was just released today."

Denim opened the CD and placed it into the CD player and pushed play. The music filled the room and like clockwork, Denim started dancing around the room.

"Patrice, this CD is better than his last one. Your boy has stepped up his game."

She danced around for a few minutes and then

said, "I'm sick of dancing by myself, Patrice. You know you need to get up out of that bed so you can start losing that baby weight."

Denim giggled and did a spin move before sitting on the side of the bed. She leaned down close to Patrice's ear and whispered, "Dré's back in town and, girl, we can barely keep our hands off each other.

"I know you're probably wondering why Dré had to leave town. If you wake up, I can tell you all about it. I'm so glad he's back. It feels so good to be in love. You know, like you and DeMario. That man misses you so much, and he won't name the baby until you wake up, so snap to it. Wake up!"

Denim thought she saw Patrice's eyes blink, but when she called her name, nothing happened.

"Patrice, you are going to be so behind in your homework. I hope you don't expect me to do some of your work for you. Now, I might type a few papers for you, but you have to do the research. You know we made a pact to graduate together, so wake up so we can plan our graduation party."

Still no sign of life from Patrice, except the sound of her breathing.

"Dang, Patrice! What is it going to take? You're starting to make me mad. Okay, I give up! Girl, do you know how hard I've been praying for you? Stop being so damn stubborn and wake up!" Denim yelled.

No response from Patrice. Denim climbed off the bed and walked over to the window. As she looked outside, tears streamed down her face. She walked back over to Patrice and pulled a tissue out of the box on the nightstand and wiped her eyes.

"I don't know what else to do, sis. I love you. I really do. Watching you lay here has been the hardest thing I've ever had to go through. If you're waiting for me to apologize, I've done it a million times. If you want to hear it again, here goes. I'm so sorry I wasn't around to help you when you were pregnant. I'm sorry I didn't have the courage to admit that I was a fool, but I'm here now, Patrice. I'm here," she pleaded as she laid her head on Patrice's chest and sobbed.

Patrice's eyes briefly fluttered; however, Denim missed it.

When she sat up, she stared down at the face of her best friend for life. "You're going to be a great mother, and I'm going to be right there to help you, but you have to wake up first. Please!"

Her cell phone rang, interrupting her. She walked over to the window. "Hello?"

"Denim, this is Felicia. I was just checking on you. I wanted to let you know we're on our way. We should be there in about twenty minutes."

Denim glanced over at Patrice, who looked like she was sleeping peacefully. "We're fine. We've been dancing and doing a lot of girl talk."

Felicia laughed. "Sounds good. I'll see you shortly."

"Yes, ma'am," Denim replied before hanging up the phone. She slipped her cell phone back into her pocket then sat on the side of Patrice's bed.

"Your little man is on his way to see you. His little chubby cheeks are so irresistible. I can't help but kiss him. Now, before you get mad, I'm not talking about DeMario, so calm down," she said with a laugh.

Denim closed her eyes and said a very personal prayer. Once she had finished, she opened her eyes and saw Patrice's eyelids flutter rapidly.

"I saw that, Patrice!" she yelled as she jumped off the side of the bed. "You can hear me, can't you? Oh my God! Oh my God! Come on! You can do it."

Denim went into a slight panic as she ran out into the hallway and called for a nurse.

Chapter Thirteen

When Felicia arrived at Patrice's room, she almost had a heart attack when she noticed the neurologist and two nurses hovering over Patrice. Denim stood over in the corner, watching the doctors so attentively that she didn't notice that Felicia had arrived.

"What's happening to my daughter?" she yelled as she set the baby's car seat in a nearby chair.

Denim ran over to her and smiled. "It's okay, Mrs. Felicia. Patrice opened her eyes!"

"She did? Oh my God!" she yelled with relief. "Have you called her father?"

"Yes, ma'am. I told him. He and DeMario are on their way."

Felicia hugged Denim before picking up her grandson. She kissed his cheek and said, "Sweetheart, your momma's awake and she can't wait to see you."

The neurologist put his stethoscope around his neck and smiled. "Your daughter is awake, Mrs. Fontenot."

Felicia glanced over at Patrice and asked, "How is she doing, doctor?"

"Everything looks good so far. She's alert and trying to talk, but I asked her not to until we get her downstairs and run some tests. I want to do another CT scan on her, as well as run some blood tests. Her vitals are good, but until we complete the tests, we won't know if there's any neurological damage. Patrice has been unconscious and had a violent seizure. We just want to be sure before we move forward."

"Are you saying my daughter could have brain damage?"

The neurologist put his hands up and said, "Calm down, Mrs. Fontenot. I'm not saying that's Patrice's case, but I want you to be aware of all the possibilities."

"I appreciate that," she answered as she looked over at Patrice.

"So far, so good, Mrs. Fontenot. I haven't seen

anything that would have me concerned about Patrice's recovery, but I'll know more once I get the results of her CT scan and other tests."

Felicia swallowed the lump in her throat and hugged the neurologist.

"You're welcome, but I can't take all the credit," he acknowledged as he looked over at Denim. "Patrice has had some great support and prayers from her family and friends. I'm very optimistic that everything is fine."

She nodded and then kissed her grandson once more before taking him over to see his mother.

Felicia watched tears flow out of her daughter's eyes. She placed the baby in Patrice's arms. Patrice was still very weak, so Felicia had to help her wrap her arm around him.

Denim was emotionally overwhelmed as she watched Patrice slowly caress her son's tiny face.

"He's beautiful, isn't he, sweetheart?" Felicia asked as she kissed Patrice's forehead and then the baby's cheek.

Patrice nodded as tears continued to flow down her face. It was then that Patrice's eyes met Denim's. Denim held her breath as she stared back at Patrice. Seconds later, a faint smile appeared on

Patrice's face as she held her hand out to Denim. Relieved, Denim slowly approached the bed and took Patrice's hand into hers.

DeMario ran from the parking lot and nearly knocked Denim down when he turned the corner in the hallway.

"Slow down, DeMario!" she yelled.

"Where's Patrice?" he asked as he tried to catch his breath.

Patrice took him by the hand and led him into Patrice's room. "They took her downstairs for some tests. She'll be back in a second."

"Cool," he answered as he looked over and saw Felicia feeding the baby.

"Where's Mr. Fontenot?" Denim asked as she looked toward the door.

DeMario stroked his son's cheek and said, "He's too slow. I left him downstairs."

At that moment, Alvin walked into the room with a scowl on his face. "Boy, do you know you almost got hit by a truck in the parking lot? It looked like it missed you by a couple of inches."

"At least I was already at the hospital if it had hit me," he replied.

Alvin sat down and gathered his thoughts. "Felicia, how's Patrice? Is she really awake?"

"Yes, honey, she's really awake."

He smiled and looked down at the baby. "How's my grandson?"

"He's fine, just greedy."

"Let me feed him," he requested as he held out his hands.

Felicia passed the baby over to Alvin and then walked out into the hallway to see if Patrice was on her way back to her room. "I thought she would've been back by now."

DeMario joined Felicia at the door. He turned and asked, "Did Patrice ask for me?"

"The doctor didn't want her to talk until he finished running all the tests. I'm sure she can't wait to see you," she assured him. "Relax, son. It looks like the worst is past us now."

DeMario sat down next to Denim and asked, "Did you call Dré?"

"Yeah, but I got his voicemail. I left him a message, so hopefully he'll be here or call me back soon."

Alvin set the baby bottle on the table and stood to burp him. He looked over at DeMario and said,

"If you had been more concerned about my daughter twelve months ago, we wouldn't even be here."

DeMario gave Alvin a heated glare, and the room immediately became so quiet that you could hear a pin drop.

"Alvin!" Felicia yelled. "This is not the time. Apologize to him!"

"No! I almost lost my daughter because of him. It's his fault, and it's time somebody let him know it."

Denim's eyes widened in surprise because she felt like a hurricane was about to hit.

DeMario stood and walked over to Alvin and calmly said, "Could you please give me my son?"

Felicia stood between the two of them because she had no idea where the confrontation was going to lead.

"No, I'm burping him," Alvin replied.

"Mr. Fontenot, please don't make me ask you again."

Alvin frowned and asked, "What did you say?"

DeMario just stared at him. It was obvious that he was showing restraint.

Denim walked over to DeMario and said, "Come on, DeMario. Let's take a walk."

"I'm not going anywhere without my son!" he

yelled, startling Denim. She'd seen him angry before, but never like this.

"Alvin, give him the baby!" Felicia yelled. "You're acting like a fool."

He reluctantly handed the baby to DeMario and sat down, mumbling under his breath.

Felicia had been strong for her family and held in her emotions for months. The altercation between her husband and DeMario had opened the flood gates, and she was livid.

"You should be ashamed of yourself, Alvin. Patrice wouldn't want you two acting like this and you know it. Our daughter just woke up from a coma, and now you want to act a fool? What's wrong with you? You know Patrice's illness was nobody's fault, and as far as her getting pregnant, get over it! We have a grandson now, and there's nothing anybody can do about it but love him," Felicia yelled.

Alvin pointed at DeMario, and with his voice cracking, yelled, "He took advantage of my daughter!"

"No, he didn't, and if you want to point fingers, why don't you start with your daughter? She loves DeMario and because of it, they, not DeMario by himself, *they* created this child! I'm so disappointed in you right now, I can't even think straight."

"I'm sorry, Felicia," Alvin mumbled.

She pointed at DeMario and said, "I'm not the one you need to be apologizing to. Don't you know that boy loves Patrice?"

"They don't know what love is!" he replied.

Felicia folded her arms and said, "I guess you would be happier if she had gotten mixed up with some dope-dealing thug."

"Of course not."

"Then squash it! DeMario's in school and working to take care of this baby. That has to account for his character."

Alvin shook his head in disbelief. "He has a job that I helped him get!"

"Would you have it any other way? He's the father of your grandson. You should want to help him, Alvin."

DeMario and Denim stepped out into the hallway to wait for Patrice. Denim put her arm around his shoulders and whispered, "Be cool, DeMario. I know you're pissed, but stay focused on Patrice and your son."

"He's crazy."

"You can't call the man crazy, DeMario."

"Why not?" he replied as he caressed his sleeping son's back. "He started this, not me, and frankly,

I couldn't care less if he likes me or not. All I care about is Patrice and our son."

"This waiting is killing me. She should've been back by now."

Seconds later, Denim and DeMario watched as technicians rolled Patrice's bed down the hallway. DeMario met them halfway and without hesitation, he leaned down and kissed Patrice on the lips. "I love you."

Patrice mouthed the words *I love you too*. Tears filled his eyes as he followed Patrice's bed into the room.

She was awake and groggy, but not too groggy to hold her baby and DeMario. The doctor didn't want her to tire herself out, so he asked the family to limit their time with her.

"Hey, guys, I'm getting ready to head out and let you guys catch up. I'll check in with you tomorrow."

Felicia hugged and kissed Denim's cheek before allowing her to leave. DeMario walked Denim to the elevator and hugged her.

"I want to thank you for keeping me from going ballistic on Patrice's dad."

"Somehow, some way, you guys are going to have to work this thing out."

"Yeah, I know, but you saw him. He's a trip."

"Yeah, but your son is his grandson, which means you're in it for life."

"I know. I'll see you later."

The doors of the elevator opened, and Denim stepped inside and pushed the button for the lobby. "Good-bye," she said as the elevator doors closed.

When Denim got outside, she opened her diary and wrote two sentences:

Dear Diary,
    Patrice FINALLY woke up and I couldn't be happier. God is good all the time.

Later,
D

After closing the diary, she dialed Dré's phone again, and this time, he picked up.

"Hey, Denim, sorry I haven't had a chance to return your call."

"So, you did get my message?"

"Yeah, I got it. I'm so glad Patrice is awake. My dad had to testify in court today."

"How did it go?" Denim asked.

"Okay, I guess. After he finished his testimony, I left."

"You didn't talk to him?"

"We talked for a few minutes before he testified. I just wanted him to see a friendly face in the audience to make it easier for him."

"Did your mom go with you?"

"Nah, she don't want to go anywhere near him right now, so I went instead."

"That's sweet of you, Dré."

"He is my dad. Now, tell me about Patrice."

Denim was like a chatterbox as she gave Dré the play by play of how Patrice woke up. Then she had the unfortunate task of telling him about the argument between DeMario and Patrice's dad.

"You had to be there, Dré. Mr. Alvin was blaming DeMario for Patrice being in a coma. It was terrible."

"Snap! For real?"

"DeMario was actually calm. I mean, I could tell he was pissed, and it was a little tense for a minute, until Mrs. Felicia started going off on Mr. Alvin."

"I'm glad I wasn't there. I don't know if I could've been as calm as DeMario."

"My heart was in my throat. If Mr. Alvin hadn't been holding the baby, I think they would've taken a swing at each other."

"That's messed up. So, where are you?" Dré inquired.

"I'm actually on my way home. It's been a long day."

"After all that drama, I guess so."

"Do you want to come over later?" she offered.

"I thought you were tired."

She giggled. "I'm not that tired."

He smiled and said softly, "I'd like that. I should be back in town in a couple of hours."

"Good. In that case, why don't you just stay for dinner?"

"If it's okay with your parents, I'm there. See you soon. I love you."

"I love you too, sweetheart," she replied.

Chapter Fourteen

Dré sat down to dinner with Denim and her family for the first time in a long time, while DeMario sat with Patrice and continued to rejoice over her recovery and their son.

"What do you think about him, Patrice? Isn't he fly?"

She reached over and caressed her son's cheek and whispered, "He's perfect."

"So, what do you want to name him?" he asked.

She frowned and said softly, "You haven't named him yet?"

"Nah, I was waiting on you to wake up so we could do it together."

"I'm sure I would've loved whatever you pick, DeMario," she replied.

"Are you mad?" he asked.

"No, I'm not mad, but he needs a name. What about Alejandro? We talked about that name before, and I really like it."

He kissed her hand and said, "Alejandro it is. Now, what about the rest of his name?"

"Well, my mom's maiden name was Chemelle. I'd like to use that as his middle name if that's okay with you."

"That works for me, baby."

"Alejandro Chemelle González. It has a nice ring to it."

DeMario looked up at her with surprise. "You want him to have my last name?"

"He's your son, isn't he?" she asked with a frown on her face.

"Yeah, but I—"

"*But I* nothing. I wouldn't have it any other way."

He kissed her lovingly on the lips and asked, "Do you know how much I love you?"

"Of course I do," she answered and then whispered softly into her son's ear. "I love you, Alejandro."

After a long nap, Patrice woke up and asked, "Did my parents go home?"

A strange expression appeared on DeMario's

face as he stood and walked over to the window. "Yeah, they went home. They wanted to give us some private time together. I think your mom will be back later tonight."

Patrice noticed DeMario's solemn expression and asked, "What's going on? Is everything okay?"

He walked back over to her bedside and smiled to reassure her. "Everything's fine."

"Everything's fine, huh?" she asked as she played with the large black curls on her son's head.

DeMario kissed her.

"I missed your kisses," Patrice whispered.

"I know that's right," he said as he took the baby out of her arms. "Rest. I don't want you straining your voice until you're stronger."

She watched as DeMario placed their son into the stroller so he could go to sleep. He reclined the seat and tucked him in with a warm blanket.

"I can't wait to get out of here. Me and Denim have lot of shopping and gossip to catch up on. I was so glad to see her when I woke up. You know she's my best friend."

DeMario looked at Patrice without responding. Something wasn't right, but he didn't want to become alarmed, so he brushed off his suspicions.

"Best friends, huh? I didn't know that," he joked.

"You're silly. You know we've never been apart since we were little. She's like a sister to me. . . . No, she's more than a sister to me; she's my soul sister and I love her. I don't know what I would do if I lost her friendship."

DeMario's heart thumped in his chest. His suspicions were starting to become a reality and it scared him. To be sure, he decided to put Patrice to the test.

"Have you guys ever had a fight?"

"Please! No! We're like twins and you know it."

"You sure are," he replied. "Do you remember the day you got sick?"

Patrice thought for a moment in silence. DeMario watched her facial expression change from happiness to confusion.

"No, but I remember Denim bringing me to the hospital. It's a little fuzzy, but I know she was there for me. That's what friends do. Right, baby?"

His suspicions were now facts. "Yeah, Patrice, that's what friends do. Now, get some rest. We'll talk more about everything later."

DeMario lowered Patrice's bed so she could get some sleep. As soon as she closed her eyes, he pulled out his cell phone and sent Denim a text message: *I need to talk 2u asap, but I'll call you. I can't talk right now. DeMario.*

Denim immediately texted him back: IS ANYTHING WRONG?

DeMario texted her once more: SORT OF, BUT IF WE PLAY OUR CARDS RIGHT, EVERYTHING WILL BE COOL.

Denim texted a response: OK. HAVING DINNER WITH THE FAMILY AND DRÉ. I'LL WAIT FOR YOUR CALL.

DeMario closed his cell phone and closed his eyes. Denim needed to know that Patrice didn't remember the breakup of their friendship. They would have to handle this situation very, very delicately.

Denim showed Dré the text from DeMario.

"I wonder what's up," he said as she picked up the dish towel.

"I don't know, but he said as soon as possible. If anything serious was going on, he would've called by now."

Dré put some soap suds on the tip of Denim's nose and said, "Okay, Cocoa Princess, are you ready to wash?"

"I am if you're ready to dry," she replied with a smile.

Dré looked over his shoulder to see if Patrice's parents were in the vicinity. "Kiss me?" he whispered.

Denim wrapped her arms around his shoulders and kissed him lovingly on the lips.

"Yummy!" he responded. "Now, get busy busting those suds."

"You just worry about drying them."

Dré got down in position like he was a quarterback waiting for the ball. "I'm ready, baby."

Denim giggled as she washed the first dinner plate and handed it to Dré to dry.

Felicia and Alvin Fontenot returned to the hospital to see Patrice and to bring some of Alejandro's belongings. When Alvin walked in, DeMario didn't even acknowledge his presence.

"How is she?" Felicia whispered as she removed her jacket.

DeMario motioned for her to step outside while Alvin checked on Alejandro.

Concerned, she asked, "What's wrong?"

"I'm not one hundred percent sure, but I think Patrice is having some memory problems."

"What makes you think that?" Felicia asked as she peeped inside the room.

"She doesn't remember the end of her friendship with Denim. She talked about how they have been inseparable since they were little, and she said she don't know what she would do if anything happened between them.

"I believe she's also getting her first hospital visit confused with this one. She thinks Denim brought her to the hospital and basically thinks Denim has been by her side the whole pregnancy. She never mentioned anything about them not speaking this past year."

Felicia put her hand over her mouth and said, "The neurologist said it was possible that she could have some memory problems, but I didn't expect this. Does Denim know?"

"I sent her a text message earlier, but I wasn't able to explain everything to her. I was waiting until you got here before I called her."

"You did good, DeMario," she replied as she put her arm around his shoulders. "You call Denim, and if I need to talk to her, I will."

"Yes, ma'am."

Felicia pushed the door to Patrice's room open and then stepped back. She turned to DeMario and said, "Listen, I'm sorry about Alvin's behavior earlier today. He was out of line."

DeMario put his hands up to stop her. "Thank you, Mrs. Felicia, but it's not your place to apologize."

"Give him a little more time. He'll eventually come around."

"All I care about is Patrice and Alejandro. Anything else is secondary."

"Alejandro? So you've named him?" she asked.

"Yes, ma'am. We named him Alejandro Chemelle González."

"You used my maiden name. That's so thoughtful of you and Patrice."

"It was Patrice's idea, Mrs. Felicia."

"Well, I'm proud of you. Now, call Denim."

Felicia returned to Patrice's bedside while De-Mario went into the waiting room to call Denim. After explaining Patrice's memory loss to Denim, she agreed not to reveal anything about their feud. In fact, Denim was happy that Patrice had somehow lost that part of her memory.

As days passed and Patrice regained her strength, she was released from the hospital. In talking more to her, DeMario also found out that Patrice had no memory of the drama surrounding Dré's family. Now that Dré was back, they saw no need to say anything to her about that, either, unless she asked or her memory started coming back to her.

Patrice had made a huge recovery and was working with a physical therapist to regain the strength in her legs and arms. Denim also helped out, since she worked in the field.

DeMario and Alvin Fontenot still hadn't settled their differences, but they were at least cordial to each other.

Denim and Patrice were inseparable once again, and Denim spent most of her afternoons with Patrice. She had cut back her days at the physical therapy clinic to three times a week, so she could regain her position on the cheerleading squad.

On this particular day, Dré, Denim and DeMario were all over at Patrice's house to celebrate Alejandro's three-month birthday. After eating a cake Patrice attempted to make, the four of them decided to play a game of Spades. They were back together like they used to be.

In the middle of the card game, Dré's cell phone rang, interrupting them.

"Hello?"

"Dré, something's happened. Turn on the TV," his mother yelled through the phone.

"Slow down, Momma. What's wrong?"

His remark caught his friends' attention. De-Mario asked, "What's going on Dré?"

DeMario turned on the TV, and they saw breaking news scrolling across the screen.

"I'm watching it now, Momma. I'll call you back," Dré said before hanging up the telephone. "Turn it up, DeMario."

The four of them watched intently as the reporter announced the news:

"Once again, if you're just joining us, a shooting occurred inside Harrier County Federal Courtroom today during the trial of accused murderer Clarence Notelli, known on the streets as C-Note. Mr. Notelli was on trial for the murder of undercover federal agent Jamal Gilbert, who was shot to death over a year ago during an undercover operation.

"Sources tell us that after the judge handed down his sentencing, shots rang out, striking Mr. Notelli and others who were thought to be associated with the murder. Neither the names of the victims nor their condition have been released; however, an officer speak-

ing anonymously did say that fatalities were involved.

"We will report more information to you as it becomes available. Now back to your regular programming."

Dré immediately called his mother back. "Momma, have you heard from Daddy?"

"No, and I can't get Agent Miller on the telephone either. Oh, Dré, I'm so sorry. I never wanted anything bad to happen to your father."

Dré's heart was pounding in his chest. He tried to remain calm for his mother's sake, but it was difficult. "Don't worry; I'm sure Daddy's fine. You keep trying to reach Agent Miller and I'll keep trying to get hold of Daddy."

Dré could hear his mother sobbing as he hung up.

"Dré, is your dad okay?" Denim asked as she hugged his waist.

"I don't know, and that's the problem. I have to go," he said as he grabbed his jacket and headed for the door.

DeMario jumped up and said, "I'm going with you."

Just as they opened the door, his cell phone rang. He quickly answered it.

"Dré, it's your dad. I'm okay."

His knees buckled, causing him to slide down to the floor. He let out a breath and said, "Where are you?"

"I'm on the move. C-Note is dead, and so are the two men who helped him murder that agent."

Tears ran down Dré's face. "What happened?"

Garrett went on the tell Dré that the teenage son of the federal agent who was murdered had somehow gotten into the courtroom with the firearm and gunned down all three men.

"Momma is freaking out. You have to call her. She's been blowing up Agent Miller's voicemail, but she wasn't getting an answer."

"Are you sure she wants to hear from me?" he asked his son.

"Yeah, I'm sure. As a matter of fact, hold on; I'm going to put her on three-way."

Dré dialed his home and listened as his father spoke softly over the telephone to his mother. During their conversation, Dana told Garrett to come home—for good. Dré now knew that his parents would be back together and they could get on with their lives, especially since C-Note and his associates were out of the picture.

He hung up his cell phone, but continued to sit on the floor.

Denim knelt down and kissed him tenderly on the lips. "From what I heard, your dad's okay?"

He pulled her into his arms and said, "Yeah, he's okay."

DeMario clapped his hands together and smiled. "I'm glad that ended well. Now, can we get back to our card game so me and my baby can whip up on you guys?"

"Sounds like a plan to me," Dré replied as he got up off the floor and took his seat at the table.

Just as the next hand was shuffled and distributed, Alejandro began to cry. Patrice stood, but DeMario stopped her.

"Sit down, babe. I'll get him."

Epilogue

Six months later, Denim sat in the neighborhood deli on her lunch break. It was Saturday, and she was working a full day at the clinic. As she ate her corned beef on wheat, looking over study material for the ACT test, three girls came into the deli and sat in the booth behind her. She ignored them until she heard one of them mention a familiar name.

"It doesn't matter!" the girl yelled. "Patience deserves payback for what she did."

This bit of information immediately caught Denim's attention.

"Don't you mean what she didn't do?" one of the girls asked.

"What are you guys talking about? This doesn't make any sense to me. Patience is the head of B.G.R. What did she do that was bad?"

One girl thumped the other girl's forehead and said, "Stop talking so loud."

"Ouch! I'm just asking! You don't have to get physical."

Denim didn't know if these girls were stupid or just didn't care who heard them plotting against the leader of their gang. In any case, Denim realized she was placed at the right place at the right time to hear what she was hearing.

"Patience knows exactly what she did. She lives with it every day. In fact, I don't know how she lives with herself."

"Are you saying you wouldn't have done the same thing if you were in her shoes?"

"What I'm saying is if you call yourself Queen of the Yard, you have to live up to that claim, no matter who gets in your face."

"You say that now, but I don't know. Patience has never shown me any fear."

"You weren't there! I saw it with my own eyes!"

"Calm down and lower your voice."

"All I know is that payback is going to be sweet, and I can't wait to see her face. I used to think that Patience was cool until—well, you know, until she showed me otherwise."

"Are y'all going to tell me what she did?"

"No!" two of the girls said in unison.

"Well, does it have something to do with the Supreme Divas gang?"

The two girls laughed.

"Well? Does it?"

"It has to do with loyalty and trust. That's all you need to know for now. We'll tell you the rest later."

"Sounds like you're the ones who have an issue with loyalty and trust. We're B.G.R. We're sisters, and we're supposed to take care of our own, not go against them."

"That's my point exactly. That's why we have to see this thing through. Agreed?"

"Agreed," the other girl answered.

"But what if she finds out about your plan? Do you have any idea what will happen to us?"

"Nothing is worse than what she put me through. I won't get over it until I get my revenge. Patience will have to pay and pay dearly."

"Does she know who you really are?"

"No, but she'll find out in due time," she said with a laugh.

The waitress came over to the table where the B.G.R. girls were sitting so she could take their orders. They ordered a large basket of chicken tenders, fries, and sodas before continuing their conversation.

Denim had heard enough. The dilemma she had now was what she was going to do with the information. It wasn't like Patience was her friend, but she had helped her in her time of need.

Denim grabbed her belongings and wrapped up her sandwich and immediately left the deli. When she climbed in her car, she sat there for a moment to gather her thoughts before driving in the direction of Scotland Heights, a high crime area and infamous B.G.R. and Supreme Divas gang territory.